FIFTH ERA

MATTHEW B. THOMPSON

ISBN-10: 0-9906276-5-9
ISBN-13: 978-0-9906276-5-4

DEDICATION & ACKNOWLEDGEMENTS

To my wife, my mother, my sister, my brother, Steve, Kate, Marge, Arliss, Ryan and Zack. You have all encouraged me more than you realize.

I am very grateful to wife, Lori, who guided my thoughts and helped me edit the book. I am also grateful to my editor, Dawn Boeck, who was able to dedicate her time and effort to helping me complete this book. I also want to deeply thank English teachers I had in Junior High School and High School. They were constantly in my mind as I typed.

I used several elements of American Pop Culture, including creations of George Lucas, Steven Spielberg, Melissa Matheson, Michael Grais and Mark Victor. Another bit of American Pop Culture are the many brand names under Kellog's. Finally, a multitude of Google's features were extremely helpful in writing this book.

Book 1 of
The Republic of Mars:

Fifth Era

MATTHEW B. THOMPSON

It's helpful to read
the glossary first.
(Uncommon words.)

CONTENTS

Chapter 1
The Battle Of Los Angeles
February 25, 1942

In 1916, Woodrow Wilson promised the American people that he would keep America out of the war in Europe. Once elected, though, he took America INTO that war and tilted the European balance of power. Prior to that time, only Europeans had shaped Europe. After the war, Wilson-influenced politics destroyed the German economy and guaranteed a 2nd World War which would require an ultimate weapon. Without Wilson's 'fib', the German economy would not have been devastated, the Nazis would not have risen to power and the Weimar Republic might still exist. There would not have been World War II, the Holocaust, the nuclear bomb or any of the other nuclear programs in the world. An old proverb talks about the road to hell . . . and how it's paved.

Sitting at a console on the front-left side of the small craft, the young blond haired, blue eyed helmsman turns his head slightly to speak. "They're firing at us, Sir." Untroubled by this, he turns back to his numerous viewscreens.

An older man sits in the center of the small vessel; behind the young helmsman, and in front of the communications officer. He has a neatly trimmed white beard and white hair. He sits forward in his chair.

Both of them are his eyes and ears, since he has no viewscreen of his own. "I'm amazed they even know we are here," he says, his deep voice resonating. He doubtingly asks, "They have weapons that can reach us?"

"Yes, Sir," says the handsome young man. "Effective ones. They'd bring us down if we were hit." Even though the helmsman looks to be only 20 years old, he handles himself like a veteran pilot.

"They've made amazing progress since my last visit, Percival," he says in a low voice. "Just evade," he orders. "We don't want to hurt them," he says. "Maneuver: Pidima. The bouncing maneuver will work just fine."

"Yes, K'kul," he answers and presses a few buttons.

Sitting behind the older man's left shoulder, the young communications officer chimes in. "Sir, we are receiving a message from L'lith's ship. Text only."

The older man sighs loudly and rubs his forehead like he has a headache. "Yes?" he asks quietly.

The communications officer reads the text, "We have detected strange radiation signatures and are investigating further."

K'kul takes a deep breath then says, "Break formation and head toward the main ship. Tell them that I am coming aboard."

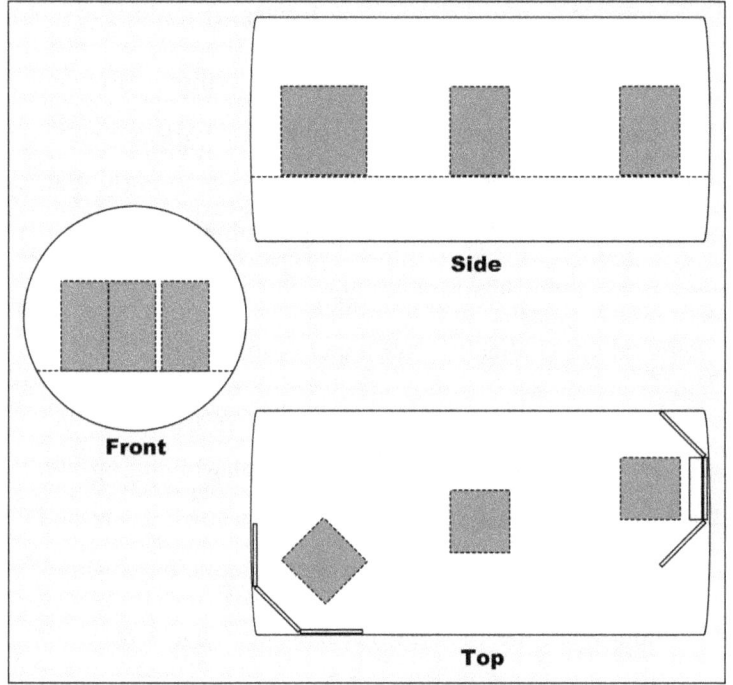

Modern Vimana

The small vessel maneuvers away from the two dozen other silvery vessels, then silently flies toward a dark form, a very **large** form, hovering in the darkness. Beginning the landing sequence; their electromagnetic sensors seem to remove the blackness, as they reveal every detail of the goliath vessel in front of them.

A circular ship isn't unusual to Percival, even if it looks like the head of a giant Tesla Coil, but the sheer size of the ship never ceases to amaze him. Knowing the exact dimensions does not make the scene any less incredible.

The blue and black mottled pattern covering the top and bottom sections constantly changes, like it's a living creature. The middle section is dark gray in color and fairly flat, allowing for landing bays and various equipment. One bay opens its twin doors and a welcoming blue light appears.

Percival automatically plots a course toward it.

The viewscreen's image grows and grows as the small vessel approaches the giant ship, like an ant walking up to a watermelon. The small vessel slips past the twin doors and blue signal lights, revealing a cavernous docking bay inside.

Without a second thought, Percival maneuvers the craft into the immense docking bay and the welcoming blue lights change to become 'unavailable' red lights.

Tall and slender, K'kul stands and impatiently waits for the craft to land. He's wearing a light gray suit-like garment, and a red cummerbund with dangling tips. The instant the small craft touches down, he steps through and disappears through the door.

K'kul stomps into a conference room with three men and a woman standing in front of a large viewscreen hanging on the wall. A table sits in the middle of the room. Even from behind, he recognizes each of them instantly. The four immediately stop talking, like it had been a private conversation that he shouldn't hear.

Ignoring their silence, "What's going on, L'lith?" he bellows.

A stunningly beautiful woman turns her head to face him; her long red hair brushes her shoulders lightly.

K'kul averts his eyes.

"'Hello' to you, too, K'kul," she replies quickly.

He purses his lips, forces himself to remain calm and politely asks, "What did you find?"

"We were waiting for you," she tells him. Her draping skirt brushes the floor. Split in the front, the overside is black while the underside is blue. Her long cape stops short of the floor, again with a black overside and blue underside.

Two of the men seem to revive from a trance while the third, a very tall and muscular man, lurks near the woman.

K'kul looks at the three men, "R'ma . . . M'kul . . . P'al . . . good to see you."

Slender and handsome, the two normal-height men radiate intelligence and strength like sunshine. R'ma has black hair, wearing the same light gray suit-like garment, but has an olive green cummerbund with dangling tips. M'kul has shoulder-length blond hair, and wears the same type of clothing, but has a pale blue cummerbund with dangling tips. P'al, the giant man, has short-cropped brown hair and a chin goatee, wearing black battle armor and a very long black cape with a blue underside, similar to the woman's.

She walks slowly toward the viewscreen. "As I said, I was waiting for everyone to arrive first." The viewscreen comes to life on its own, displaying technical data and charts. "We detected a strange radiation coming from one of their cities."

Unmoved by either her beauty or her delays, "And?" K'kul asks impatiently. "What is it?" he demands.

The woman ignores his irreverent tone. "They are making plutonium," she says flatly.

Speechless, the four stand in silence like they'd heard about a friend's death. K'kul slowly backs up and sits at the table.

Anticipating his next question she calmly replies. "We're sure," she says. "The scans are conclusive."

The others stand in silence, as if at a funeral. Emotionless, she sits at the table while her words seem to echo through their minds. The others follow suit, as though waiting for her cue.

The silence echoes through the room for several seconds.

All of them are shaken by the news. "I knew their technology would advance quickly," one of the men quietly says, "but I didn't think they'd advance **this** quickly."

"None of us did, R'ma," K'kul says. He turns to the woman. "Is it coming from Los Angeles?"

"No," she answers. "It's from further up the coast."

"We can't monitor on them every thirty years anymore," K'kul insists. "It has to be done sooner now."

"The more we interfere with their progress, the more we shackle them," the blond man warns.

"They are advancing much faster than we expected, M'kul," K'kul counters. "Our nets are too wide. They're spiraling."

"Are they spiraling downwards or spiraling upwards?" she asks.

K'kul shoots a look at her. "Technology and wisdom must keep pace with each other," he tells her with his deep baritone voice. "If technology outpaces wisdom by too much, then the society will spiral downward . . . rapidly. It always does."

She scoffs. "Then **give** them wisdom," she answers.

"Wisdom comes with experience," M'kul explains. "We can't give them failures and successes."

R'ma ignores the squabble, pushing the topic aside. "Plutonium has only one **real** use," he says. "We should monitor them yearly, and prevent the other side from developing more serious technologies."

M'kul is shocked. "Yearly?!" he exclaims.

K'kul bellows at the same time. "Neural omissions again?!"

R'ma answers both men. "Solar years, M'kul, not lunar ones. K'kul, no need to jump to conclusions. This is not Heron of Alexandria or Aristocles all over again. We'll use a simpler and much more palatable strategy."

The woman cuts in. "These people are becoming more and more connected to each other," she recognizes. "They spread their knowledge before we can get to them. Neural omissions are no longer effective."

Silent until now, a deep and guttural voice imposes. "Destroy it again?"

"No," K'kul answers. "That didn't work 30 years ago. They found a way around it. L'lith is right. This world is becoming smaller with each passing year."

"Yes," R'ma adds.

K'kul continues. "If we allow them to continue this project, it will stop itself."

M'kul doubts him. "How do you figure that?" he asks.

"This is an ultimate weapon," he answers matter-of-factly. "If no one else can counter it with something more advanced, they'll win the war and this whole thing will end."

"Yes," R'ma agrees. "We'll allow this technology, and stifle any new ones."

"They're clever," M'kul mutters. "Damn clever."

"Yes, they are," K'kul answers. "Burying their creation under three miles of water wasn't enough last time. Instead of destroying their creations, we should simply **take** their creations," he says. "They can't fix things they can't find."

"That includes Foreign National crashes," R'ma adds.

"Those idiots," the woman says under her breath.

R'ma hears her, but ignores it. "They're already headed for another technological revolution, but we don't want it to go too far."

"Agreed," M'kul interjects. "We need to assign men to blend into their society and constantly monitor them. Men in black, so to speak."

"We only need one person for this," the woman says. "If we just move him from place to place, people will think there's a lot of them. That'll also keep our fingerprints to a minimum, while keeping 'Control' to a maximum. We'll recruit a human from the **other** side of this war, someone very familiar with all the new technologies. Does everyone agree?" She looks around at the nodding heads.

K'kul grudgingly says, "Yes." He stands, opens the door and walks through it.

A disappointed K'kul appears at the small vessel fifteen minutes after he'd left. "Take us back, Percival," he orders.

Startled by the instruction, Percival spins his chair toward K'kul, "Sir?" he asks.

"Something's happened," he says. K'kul walks slowly across the cabin and sinks into his chair. "The Council has decided to wait . . . and I agree. We'll let this situation calm down and try again later . . . much later."

Knowing not to ask, the young man quietly says, "I see." Spinning his seat back toward the control panel, the silver vessel silently lifts off. He solemnly steers it between the massive bay doors, then back down and under the dark water.

Chapter 2
Decades Later

January, 2026

Why would a primitive culture believe that a highly advanced culture would actually LET primitives keep its technology . . . or its people?

In an Internet chat room.

```
Tex:    What do you think, Asher?
```

He's eating dinner at the computer. Asher shifts his plate off of the keyboard.

```
Asher:  Every time someone makes a prediction,
        other people always bring up the Mayan
        thing.

Asher:  They say, "It didn't happen last time, so
        why will it happen THIS time?"

Tex:    Exactly!

Tex:    Why would it?

Asher:  The 2012 prediction has NO BEARING on the
        current prediction.

Asher:  They are independent events.

Asher:  People think the Mayan thing was about the
        Apocalypse.

Asher:  I think people LOOK for things to be
        paranoid about.
```

Asher: Of course, that's more and more common these days.

Asher: I try not to think about their nonsense.

Joe: Nonsense, huh? You hadn't thought about it?

Joe: I know you're dying to tell us, so go ahead.

The three of them have been chatting on the Internet for nearly two years. Even though they all live in Washington, D.C., they've never met face-to-face. Tex got his nickname from living in Texas and Joe came from 'G.I. Joe' because he's a medic in the U.S. Army, but Asher's nickname had not been as inventive - it's just his last name.

Asher's face flushes. Luckily he safely sits on the other side of a computer screen.

Asher: Since you really want to know...

Tex: Come on. Let it out.

Asher: The Maya lived a thousand years ago and were a highly advanced civilization in Central America.

Asher: They had a calendar that was even more accurate than ours.

Tex: See? YOU feel better we're DEFINITELY better.

Tex: You're done since we're all better now.

Joe: Very funny, Tex.

Joe: But I want to hear more about it.

Joe: I like stuff like this.

Tex: And once he gets started it's hard to shut
        him up.

Asher ignores him.

Asher: OK. It's probably sounds a bit geeky. . .

Tex: No! You?

But adds before anyone explodes.

Tex: Sorry. Sorry. Couldn't help it.

Asher: Their calendar did more than just count the
        days.

Asher: They   got   information   from   previous
        civilizations   for   eclipses,   hurricanes,
        earthquakes,   births,   deaths   and   other
        stuff.

Asher: They found regular cycles in EVERYTHING and
        put that in their calendar, then used it to
        make predictions.

Asher: That   sort   of   thing   is   specific   to   the
        geographic region.

Joe has a moment of brilliance . . .

Joe: You would think that San Francisco or New
        York could do the same thing.

. . .and then it's gone.

Joe: Is this what Nostradamus did?

Asher: Nah.

Asher: Nostradamus wrote a bunch of vague stuff, then took credit for it when something happened to fit.

Tex: Like that astrology crap.

Joe: I don't know what you guys are talking about.

Joe: I follow my horoscope every day.

Tex: You would.

That did it.

Joe: AND WHAT DOES THAT MEAN?

Asher interjects, hoping to calm their tempers.

Asher: Nostradamus' real name was Michel.

Tex: Mike? That's cool!

Asher: No.

Asher: Michel, pronounced like the girl's name Michelle.

Joe: He was a woman?

Asher laughs to himself.

Asher: No.

Asher: Michel is a traditional boy's name in France.

Tex: That figures.

Tex: Hundreds of years later, he's STILL screwing with people.

Tex: I guess the French version of a badass soldier believes all that crap, too.

Joe: I'm a medic, not a soldier.

Joe: But I guess reading isn't your strong suit.

Desperately trying to defuse the situation:

Asher: Michel de Nostra-Dame flunked out of medical school and changed his name to 'Nostradamus.'

Tex: Okay, I'll bite.

Tex: Why did he change his name?

Relieved that he finally distracted them, Asher eagerly writes:

Asher: So no one would recognize the name of a flunky.

Asher: He ran around the countryside, calling himself a doctor and selling magic potions.

Tex: Didn't he write, too?

Asher: Vague stuff, yeah. It's called 'Cold Reading.'

Joe jokingly writes, getting in the conversation again.

Joe: Reading a book in the snow?

Asher-The-Egghead answers the question without missing a beat.

Asher: It's a technique for reading a person without knowing anything about them. Cold.

He realizes it's a joke as soon as he hits the 'Enter' key.

Asher: Speaking of snow, when are we going out on the town?

Asher: I just can't do weeknights.

Tex: Government worker.

Tex: I thought you government types could come to work whenever you want.

Asher: It doesn't work that way in MY office.

Asher: It was at YOUR suggestion that I go get the job.

Joe: We're both happy for you, Asher.

Joe: When we first started chatting, you were just using that big brain of yours to write computer programs in your parent's basement.

Joe: Now you're on your own and working on computers in the White House.

Asher: It's the Eisenhower Building. They're easy to confuse.

Tex: Whatever.

Tex: We're trying to give you a compliment.

Asher: Oh. I'm sorry.

Tex gets annoyed.

Tex: That's what we've been talking about.

Tex: Even though you've moved out on your own
        and gotten a great job, you still lack one
        major thing...

Tex: confidence and assertiveness.

Asher: You know that's two things, right?

Tex explodes.

Tex: Dammit! That, too!

Tex: Quit being so damn... literal!

Tex: People don't like it and women REALLY don't
        like it!

Joe breaks in so Tex can calm down.

Joe: Just be assertive, have confidence and quit
        correcting people.

Joe: That's all you need to do.

Asher sits back, thinks for a moment, then writes:

Asher: I'm not sure if I want her to remember me
        or not.

Joe: Joanne? Are you still thinking about that
        one girl?

He hangs his head, even though they can't see him.

Asher: I'm trying to improve myself for lots of reasons, but she's what I use as a gauge.

Tex: He's obsessed.

Asher rockets out a response.

Asher: I AM NOT!

Asher: I see her opinion as a high mark on the 'female opinions gauge.'

Asher: If I pass her inspection, then I'll pass ANY inspection.

Tex: He has a point.

Joe: I'm not sure how high a mark it is.

Joe: All she asked is that you don't live with your parents, have a job and act like a man.

Tex: On the first date?!

Tex: I can understand on the third, seventh or even the twentieth date.

Tex: But on the FIRST date?!

Tex: I agree with Asher. The girl's a snob.

Joe: Okay. She asked a lot of him a bit too early in their relationship.

Tex: What relationship?!

Tex: That was their FIRST date!

Joe: Fine! Fine!

Joe: The girl has issues.

Elsewhere in the World

In the pre-dawn hours, the thunderous roar of a jet engine echoes across the never-ending desert. "Cruising at 36,000 feet. Smooth as silk," Major Donnelly says on the radio.

"Continue on course three zero six," a woman's voice answers. "We'll be glad to see you two back."

Another man sits directly to his left, "After the mission we ran," he says, "you should be ecstatic to have us back. Have you heard anything from my wife? The 'due date' is almost here."

The white sands and towering dunes glint below them. A pink horizon hints of the coming dawn.

"Negative, Colonel," she answers. "But I will call and ask. These things can be a bit unpredictable."

Out of nowhere the cabin shudders. "What the hell?" Colonel Drake yells.

Alarms sound throughout the cabin, and the shudder becomes a violent upheaval. "Strap in!" he yells.

Major Donnelly catches a glimpse through the window. As if in slow motion, he sees the horizon twist to the left, then up to the sky. The violence swells into a tidal wave of ferocity, as if a massive earthquake has hit the aircraft. An invisible force shoves the two men back into their seats.

The major looks at the control panels. "The port wing's been hit!" he yells. "The computers are trying to compensate! I don't think it'll go!"

Colonel Drake yells at the radio, "Something's hit our port wing, but from above!"

"Meteor," the radio says. "Eject!"

The G-force pulls **hard**, and the Colonel grunts from the force. "Not happening!" he manages. "End over end! We're going down!"

Sitting in front of a white tent and a campfire, a Bedouin boy watches the early morning sky. A black dot catches his attention. As it grows larger, he realizes that it's a falling airplane. "Muhammad!"

An older man stumbles out of the tent. "What?" he answers. "Where is breakfast?"

The young boy points at the falling airplane. "Look!" he says.

Muhammad stares at it for a few moments then smiles. "An American airplane," he says under his breath then ecstatically calls to the others. "Everyone out!" he yells.

"Now!"

Several men slowly walk out of the tent.

"This is our chance, my friends. Allah has smiled on us. That," he says, pointing to the tumbling aircraft, "is an American airplane. It's black because it is one of their secret airplanes. Much, much gold!"

Electrified by their good luck, the group can hardly restrain themselves.

He restrains the group for a few more seconds. "We must capture it and anyone inside," he tells them. "The men are worth much more if they are alive. Let's go!" he yells. "Allah is with us!"

The men rush to their camels, yelling in excitement.

Several Hours Later

Focusing on a blip on a small screen, an American helicopter pilot talks on his radio. "Sir, the transponder's signal says it's here, but I don't see anything at all."

The mid-twenties pilot wears sunglasses and a camouflage uniform while flying above an endless ocean of sand dunes.

The raspy electronic voice of an older man answers. "It's

not like the damn thing's small, Captain." The helicopter pilot can hear a sigh over the radio. The rough, older man's voice continues. "But maybe something's broken off or hidden in the sand. In a sandstorm, things can be buried in minutes."

"Understood, Sir," the young pilot answers, both acknowledging his superior and finding solutions to the problem. "I'll set down and have the team fan out. We'll find it." As an afterthought he adds. "Sir, this isn't very encouraging for the colonel and the major."

"That's already crossed my mind, Captain," the radio answers. "Just find them!"

The pilot lands the helicopter and relays the orders. They offload, carrying metal detectors and transponder locators then start the search. "Colonel," the young pilot says over the radio, "We ran into a Bedouin group a little while ago. They seemed agitated, but I figured it was because we're foreign soldiers in a helicopter."

The Colonel scolds him. "That PC crap will get you killed, Captain," he yells. "More importantly it can get our men killed."

The helicopter pilot subconsciously hangs his head a little. "Yes, Sir," he answers and quietly sighs.

Outside the men focus on the side of one sand dune. "Sir!"

one of them yells. "We found the transponder signal and a large metal object!"

With more pep in his voice, the Captain relays the news on the radio. "Sir, they just found the transponder signal and a large metal object."

"Good, Captain," the electronic voice tells him. "With the way they went down, we don't know if they were able to eject."

Digging in the sand, the men uncover the black nose of the airplane. "We got it!"

The men quickly uncover its front window. Sgt. Aaron whips out a flashlight, scanning the cockpit's insides through it. "I don't see anyone inside, Sir!" he says.

Another soldier has been uncovering the roof of the cabin. "Sir, I don't think this was buried by the wind," he says. "The door's been opened, I don't see anyone inside and some parts are buried deep while other parts are buried shallow. I think this was intentional."

The chopper pilot head-smacked the air in front of him. "The Colonel was right," he says to himself. "It was the Bedouin group." He leans out of the chopper. "Aaron and Smith!" he yells. "Stay here and guard the aircraft! Don't uncover any more! The rest of you, climb in!" He revs the helicopter while four men clamber aboard. The two guards shield their eyes as the blades blow a stronger and stronger mini-sandstorm.

"How do you want to do this, Sir?" a soldier asks, yelling over the screaming blades.

The pilot doesn't like being fooled by a simple trick, and turns his head halfway to talk to his men. "Simple!" he yells. "I'll drop three of you off a few hundred yards away! Peretti, you'll stay with me and translate! The two of us will land and make a big deal! While they're distracted you three will go in, find the men and get them out the back! We'll give you about 20 minutes then pick you up!"

While talking to his own men, the pilot gets even angrier. "These primitives may have found the plane," he tells them, "but I guess they thought we'd **let** them keep our equipment!" He turns forwards and the helicopter lifts off. "Or our men!" he adds.

Chapter 3
Back In 2012

The FAPE law, 'All U.S. residents will receive Free and Appropriate Public Education' is simply the version of a law that people remember. Its roots go all the way back to the Emancipation Proclamation in 1863. It started with freeing slaves of any race, became a civil rights act, went through MULTIPLE revisions, was applied to disabilities, was applied to disabilities in school, became the FAPE law in 1973, and has had 3 revisions since. Progressive politicians change the law, let people get used to it, and then change it a little more. That's called 'progression.' It's not based on the word 'progress,' just like the word 'Democrat' isn't based on the word 'democracy.'

If progressive politicians were genuinely interested in progress, they'd make failure of a public school course result in the student financially paying for the course. Education and parental involvement would skyrocket. Like it or not, financial risk motivates people.

"Stella!" he screams.

A young woman appears near the man's ladder, as if summoned by magic. "George, you know that my name is 'Kim.'"

"I know," he says, smiling and laughing to himself. "Kim Hunter."

She crosses her arms. "Yeah," she says indignantly. "How do you get 'Stella' from 'Kim?'" she asks.

"Kim Hunter played Stella Kowalski," he answers.

"Was that some cop show back in the 80s?" she asks sarcastically.

He sighs, mutters something about kids these days and climbs down the store's stocking ladder. "Doesn't matter," he says. "We'll need to stock this whole aisle again".

She suddenly notices the bare aisle. "Oh my God!" she says. "What did they do with all this stuff?"

He sarcastically answers her. "They bought it."

Ignoring him, she walks partway down the aisle. "I stocked this entire aisle **yesterday**!"

"Yep," he says nonchalantly. "Partly it's Christmastime," he says while walking through the stock room doors. He comes back with an enormous teddy bear under each arm. "Partly it's this 'End of the World' baloney," he says while moving his arms or as much as he can carrying two giant teddy bears. After arranging the new bears with the last one on the shelf, he walks toward the stock room.

"What's all the excitement about anyway?" she asks.

He looks at her. "First of all," he says, "it's about you watching me work."

"Sorry," she says, and scurries to the stock room to get more stuffed animals.

When she returns, he authoritatively continues. "Well, some nitwit made a prediction that the world will end in a few days." He picks up a five-foot nutcracker soldier. "I'll get these, and you get a couple more bears." He mutters to himself. "This happens every few years or so. Some people get more publicity, and others don't. Anyway, some nitwit makes a prediction about the end of the world, based on whatever is hot right then. The nitwit gets famous for a little while. Some people like believing in that stuff, even though it never comes true."

"Why is the big and expensive stuff going so fast?" she asks.

"This also happened back in 2000," he says, carrying the large nutcracker soldiers through the door. "The Apocalypse-people think the world's going to end, so they buy big gifts for Christmas. They probably think they won't have to pay for them."

After stocking the shelf, they arrange it.

George walks back into the stock room and yells back at Kim. "It's good for business, though." Picking up another soldier, he trots back to her and says, "I feel sorry for those grocery store guys. Their customers buy loads and loads of Pop-Tarts and beer!" he laughs. He gets more and more amused, saying, "I mean . . . Do these people actually think that Pop-Tarts will save them?! I guess if Pop-Tarts don't, the beer will take the edge off!"

He laughs even harder.

In a Catholic Mass

Some parishioners are half-asleep from last night's party when a gray-haired priest shouts, "The 'End of Days' is upon us!"

Many people sit up.

It might be just a knee-jerk reaction, the priest thinks, *but at least NOW they are now paying attention.* "St. Malachy warned us of this. In 1139, he prophesied that the last pope, the Antichrist, Peter the Roman, would be the 112th pope . . . misleading the 111th pope with his beautiful, yet poisonous words. Beginning with Pope Celestine II in 1143, Pope Benedict XVI is the 111th pope. The Bible tells us that after has reins for seven years, the Antichrist will reveal himself and then destroy the Catholic Church." He pauses, letting the words sink into the minds of his parishioners.

The people murmur and shift in the pews.

"His coat of arms," the priest continues, "'De Gloria Olivae', 'The Glory of the Olive', could refer to 'The Order of Saint Benedict', his namesake . . .or it could refer to him as the 'Bringer of the Olive Branch', a peacemaker . . . or he could fulfill 'Olive's Glory' as revealed in 'The Mystical Eschatology of the Vatican' and returning 'The Keys To The Kingdom To Christ's Second Coming'. Prophecy **necessarily** lacks details."

The old priest becomes silent and bows his head. "The Antichrist is sinister," he says at last. "We all know this; it isn't a new idea."

He pauses again. "Most people think that means 'evil,' and we all say 'Of course, he's evil. He's the Antichrist!'"

He cups his chin with his hand. "Does that mean evil or does that mean left-handed?" he asks.

The parishioners murmur again.

"Or both?" he adds. "Sinister, smoke and fire, foreign-born, European ideas, talks about the olive branch . . ."

"But there is hope; Christ can **only** come after the Antichrist has reigned," he tells them somberly, "and Pope Benedict's coat of arms has two large keys hidden in the corners. The Antichrist is smart. He knows we know these secrets. His rise may be a boom or a whisper - we don't know which, but we do know that this pope served the NAZIs. Will he bring peace to the world or will he lead us into the clawed hands of the Antichrist? The Antichrist is **cunning**. Do not assume the answer . . . but don't ignore the obvious, either."

At the Same Time

A man wearing a blue shirt and khaki slacks walks into an office at a university in the state of Arizona. Another man, wearing a dark-colored suit and red tie, sits behind the desk. He has brown hair, a beard and glasses. He barely notices the visitor enter the office, as he thumbs through papers on the desk.

"Mind if I have your apple?" the visitor asks.

The man behind the desk looks up, but before he can answer, the other one snatches the apple from the desk and bites into it with a loud crunch.

"Yeah, sure," he says sarcastically and continues looking at individual papers, then puts them in his satchel. "I don't see why it's such a big deal, Richard," he says, "It's just an alignment."

"They want to make sure the sun will come back," he says and bites into the apple again. He notices all the papers on the desk. "Grading papers?" he asks. "No T.A.?"

He puts the last of the papers into his satchel. "This isn't an eclipse and no," he answers, bustling toward the door. "We found something strange on some satellite images, so I'm taking the printouts home. I hate to run out on you, but . . ."

"Press. . . I know. Just remember that reporters are like wolves," he says. "At long range they seem very mild. Maybe even gentle. At close range, they'll rip you to shreds and eat you alive."

Dr. Livingston stops at the door for a moment. "I doubt they're that bad," he says, and walks away.

Richard leans against the doorjamb. "You might get lucky," he says, "but then again . . . They're not stupid, but they're not the sharpest knives in the drawer."

Dr. Livingston hurries down the hall.

Richard walks to the doorway and shouts. "I bet you ten bucks that they ask about dinosaurs and California."

He echoes from the end of the hall. "Okay," he shouts, "You're on!"

Outside

The head of the Astronomy Department, Dr. Bill Livingston, stands amongst microphones and speaks to the cameras. "This is nothing more than an alignment," he tells them, half-blinded by camera flashes. "The Earth and Sun have aligned with the center of the galaxy every 26,000 years and has done so for four and a half **billion** years. That's more than 173 thousand times. The Earth is still here." The reporters don't seem to understand.

In the frenzy, a single person calls out. "I thought it was 640,000 years."

Bill smiles, thinking, *This will be easy.* "You've been watching too much TV. The Ancient Maya believed that the center of the galaxy was the birthplace of mankind," he tells them. "This alignment probably symbolizes a rebirth of some kind, but certainly not the end of the world. That's Christian ideology, not Mayan."

While the reporters fight each other, battling to get their question heard, he hoped for an intelligent question. No such luck.

A man's voice eclipses the others, "Dr. Livingston, what about the dinosaurs?" he asks. "Didn't an asteroid destroy their world, but not the planet? How is that different?"

Dinosaurs, he thinks. *That's not BOTH things, so I don't owe him ten bucks just yet.* "It's true that an asteroid helped to destroy them, but it's also true that we have been cataloguing and tracking objects like that for decades, for exactly that reason. We know the exact position and path of every large object crossing Earth's orbit."

"Candace Cohen from the *Tulsa Gazette*," another reporter announces. "Most objects, yes, but not all."

The reporters hush for a moment then mumble amongst themselves.

Impressed that she was able to shut up a reporter feeding frenzy like this, Dr. Livingston decides to try a softer approach with her. "You're a long way from home, Ms. Cohen," he says, smiling. "Asteroids hit each other all the time, sometimes sending one our way and sometimes breaking off chunks. We aren't in the business of assuming that we know the location of every rock in space, just like you wouldn't assume a geologist knows the location of every grain of sand on Earth. However, he **does** know where all the beaches are located, and we do the same kind of thing. Big asteroids are the dangerous ones, but those are easy to track. Earth is in no danger."

The reporters squabble amongst themselves for a few moments. *Why would anyone want a life like this?* he wonders.

A single reporter appears to ask her question. "Dr. Livingston," she says. "What about California? Can this event push it into the ocean?"

Dammit! he thinks. *She HAD to bring up California!* "I'm an astronomer, not a geologist, but my understanding is that the tectonic plates are grinding **along** each other, not **away** from each other. California's **never** going to fall into the ocean and certainly not because of an alignment."

"So as a non-geologist," she says, "you can't say 'For Sure.' Can you?"

This poor woman has wasted her life, he thinks. *And after watching a few TV shows even believes she's a top-flight attorney.* He'd like to slap this woman for spreading her stupidity, but knows that he would be the one is trouble.

Instead, he grits his teeth. "No," he answers.

Chapter 4
The Return of the Nine

For the believer, there's an over-abundance of evidence. For the non-believer, there's never enough.

At exactly 6:55 in the morning, a circular mass rises from the depths of the Catalina Channel near Los Angeles. Water doesn't even touch the bulbous object as it silently slips from the ocean's grasp. The brown circle grows larger and taller, looking like a giant turtle shell. The turtle shell grows into a brown mountain, like the ocean is birthing the horn of a new continent.

The horn is a titanic UFO, climbing up through the waves. It escapes the watery slumber without splashes, bubbles or even a hum. Released from the sea, the immense craft levitates skywards; a swirling vortex of water churns briefly beneath as it leaves. Short and thick 'wings' encircle the titanic spaceship. Suddenly, two pale white engines ignite, lurching the mountainous ship forward and toward the City of Angels.

At a nearby military base, a blip appears on a radar screen . . . a very **large** blip . . . moving very quickly across the screen. "Whoa!" the radar operator says out loud.

The other tech in the radar room sits only a few feet away in the small room. Without taking his eyes off of his own computer screen he asks, "What's up?"

He jumps off his stool and points to the screen. "You've gotta get over here and confirm this!" he yells at the tech.

Irritated with him. "Hold your horses," he says. "It's not like I'm a mile away." He walks over and looks at the screen. "Whoa!" he yells. "Confirmed! Get the C/O on the line! We've got a bogie nearly on top of us!"

Moments later, and a dozen miles from land, two F/A-18 fighter jets patrolling the skies get a radio call, changing their orders. They immediately change course and ignite their afterburners.

The leviathan reaches Long Beach in only a few minutes. It changes course and moves toward the famous area of Hollywood. The F/A-18s reach the leviathan before it gets there. The commander flips a few buttons and radios the tower. "Secure transmission to General Westin."

A supremely confident voice comes over the radio. "This is General Westin," he says. "We're secure, Commander."

"Sir," he says, "This is not your typical bogie. Look at my forward camera, and you'll see what I mean." He transmits the image.

The commander hears, "Holy Mother of God!"

"Sir," the RIO interjects, "This thing is as long as three aircraft carriers and moving like greased lightning!"

Commander Eppes tells him, "Sir, I don't think SAMs or ACUs can keep up with this thing. We're gonna need a lot more fighters up here."

General Westin takes a deep breath. "Commander," he begins, "I'm going to send every available fighter I can muster. You'll have a small army in a few minutes. We won't lose it this time!"

Commander Eppes and his wingman fly cautiously behind the leviathan, trying to hide their presence until reinforcements arrive. They don't have to wait long.

Within two minutes and from several directions F-16s, F/A-18s and even F-4 fighter jets join them. Fifteen aircrafts strong now, they move up and buzz around the silent craft like angry hornets. Minutes later, even more fighters arrive to challenge the leviathan. The hulking ship lumbers past the city, changes course to the southeast, then heads into the desert. For a split second, the fighter pilots think they've won a small victory. However, they soon realize that the monstrous ship's new direction is taking it directly to Las Vegas.

Three planes quickly fall into an attack position behind the huge vessel. They fire a barrage of bullets above it as warning shots. There is no change or response from the unknown vessel. Commander Eppes radios back to base. "Sir," he says. "We fired warning shots over its hull, but there is no response. It's broken deeper into U.S. airspace and poses a clear and present danger to civilians. Do I have permission to fire my missiles?"

General Westin's voice appears. "Commander" he replies, "as soon as you are in an unpopulated area, you have permission to fire."

"Yes, Sir," he answers. "We are nearly there now." Commander Eppes swallows with difficulty. "We're over the mountains now. Jared and Rogers, prepare to launch both of your sidewinder missiles." He says a quick prayer. "Now!" he yells. Six sidewinder missiles detach and scream toward the ship. In an instant the leviathan jumps to 5,000 miles per hour.

Stunned at first, Commander Eppes watches as six smoke streams harmlessly trail off into the clear sky. "Holy crap," he whispers.

Getting angry, he rumples his face. *Son of a. . .* he thinks. After a few choice phrases to himself, he speaks normally on the radio. "No joy, Sir," he reports. "The bogie jumped to an astonishing speed before missiles could even reach it."

Captain Jared breaks in. "It bolted like nothing I've ever seen, Sir! There wasn't even a sonic boom. That's not even possible, Sir."

The steely general answers. "Pull back for now, boys," he orders. "I've already radioed Las Vegas. This isn't over."

Near Las Vegas

Five F-22 Raptors fly in a clear blue sky over the Nevada desert. "This is not a drill, gentlemen," the lead pilot says. "Our airspace has been deeply penetrated by a hostile force. Set your weapons to hot. Permission granted by General Westin. RJ, do you see anything on the radar, yet?"

"No Sir," he answers.

"Keep your eyes peeled, Captain," he says. "We're flying straight into them. General Westin said that this thing was moving like greased lightning; and that's no joke. Ground-based radar clocked this thing at over 5,000 knots."

The captain puffs out a small laugh, "Colonel, at those speeds our onboard radars won't be able to track them for more than a few seconds. We need a ground-based feed." Then suddenly, "Whoa, Sir! Bogie at two-seven-one!"

Colonel Bratten doesn't hesitate, "All aircraft, fire your missiles!"

Time moves slowly as Captain Watson watches ten smoke plumes scream toward the leviathan. The giant ship seems to jump out of the way for an instant then back to its original course.

He blinks his eyes. "Go to guns!" he yells. Just as they start to fire, the leviathan flies straight into them. It seems to jump around as it did before, leaving five aircraft completely unscathed and completely alone.

"RJ, did you just see that?" he screams. "Did you have the video recorder on?"

"Yes Sir, I did . . . on both counts," RJ answers. "Ground has a live feed."

Never more than 3,000 feet above the ground, the leviathan continues toward the desert oasis that is Las Vegas.

In a Casino Hotel Room

From a hotel room window, a sleepy woman watches the rising sun on the desert's horizon. Still dressed from the night before, she watches at the desert's dawn. Suddenly, the giant ship streaks in front of her pleasant scene and instantly slows to a crawl.

Her eyes bulge. She blinks them a few times before looking again. She still sees it . . . slowly moving toward her. "Chuck!" she screams. "**<u>Chuck!</u>**"

"What?!" a man groggily answers from the couch. "I've been up all night. Drinking and gambling and whatever else I did. What do you want?!"

She beckons him with her hand. "Come here!" she pleads. "Quick! There's a Star Destroyer outside."

More awake now. "What??" Chuck asks, wondering if he heard her right. He stretches, gets off of the couch and lumbers to the window. "I've been awake all night, got drunk off my ass and even came over here to see your hallucination. Now what the hell do you want me to see?" he asks.

The leviathan reaches the hotel, blocking the entire horizon and passes directly overhead.

"**<u>Holy crap!</u>**" he yells, instantly awake. They both drop to the floor. They huddle together as a giant shadow passes over every hotel in sight. "That was **<u>not</u>** a Star Destroyer," he tells her.

Five fighter jets suddenly appear and streak across the sky

on full afterburners.

Chuck whispers to her. "That was only the first one," he says. "The military is involved, but can't keep up. We just saw the scout ship for an alien invasion."

In Other Parts of the Country

Denver, Lincoln and now Chicago try different attack strategies; each assault more dangerous and more deadly than the last. Even though missiles are not effective against a target moving at such extreme speeds, they are better than nothing. Fifty, a hundred, two hundred jet aircrafts from across the country join forces to fight the titanic intruder. No two planes look alike, but they all fight alike. Jet aircrafts launch barrage after barrage of missiles and bullets, but the massive ship does its bouncing maneuver and simply evades the American 'clouds of death' like they're not even there. The intruder never fires a single shot, dodging the bullets and missiles and simply continues flying toward the Windy City as if nothing has happened.

News reporters, film crews and citizens video-record the incredible scene as the massive ship flies overhead. "I can't believe it," a woman tells a reporter on camera. "I can't believe this is really happening. God help us!"

A man jumps in front of the camera. "Now do you believe us?" he asks. "We've been telling you that they're coming for years."

The woman puts her face in her hands and sobs.

"You didn't believe us then," he tells her. "You said we were crazy. Do you believe us now?!"

"I'm sorry!" the woman cries. "Help us! Please! Just help us!"

Television stations around the world interrupt their programs to break the news. "The American military is the world's strongest military," a female reporter says. "But even **they** are powerless to stop this threat. We've even heard rumors of a nuclear attack."

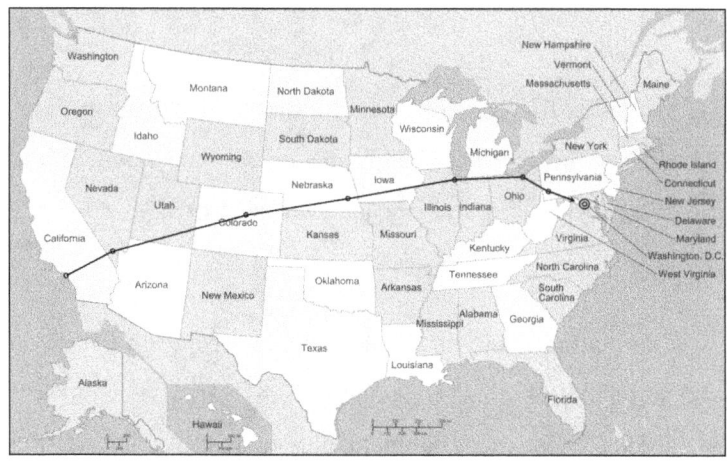

Flight Path

Inside the White House

A young soldier runs up to a general that's about to walk in to the Oval Office. The general's highly decorated uniform has six silver stars on his collar: five of them form a pentagon shape, while the sixth star is in the center.

Oh God! the young soldier gasps. *The Joint Chief of Staff Chairman!* He stiffly salutes the dark-skinned man, he says, "Cleveland failed, too, Sir. They've jumped to hyper-speed again. If they skip Pittsburgh, they'll be here in about four minutes."

"Thank you, Son," General Hamilton tells him, salutes and walks through the door.

The room is filled with people talking loudly, and all at once. They hush for a moment when the general comes in, anxious for the news.

"Cleveland's failed, gentlemen," he tells the others in the room, and the noise immediately resumes. "We have four minutes," he says, trying to be heard over the crowd.

The room gets louder.

A white-haired man with blue eyes and dressed in a dark-colored suit and a blue tie, walks up to him. "Alan, how did it go?" he asks. Obviously agitated, he nervously looks around.

The general is in his mid-fifties, clean-cut, has gold-rimmed glasses and wears a mustache. He stands at attention for a moment, salutes, then relaxes. "Not well, Mr. President," he says. "Almost two hundred fighter aircraft . . ."

General Hamilton's words fade as the President unexpectedly sits down and talks to himself. "Not good! Not good! I didn't want this job," he mutters. "I mean the perks are great, but . . ."

The general interrupts his rambling. "Sir, we still have two methods of attack," he tells him.

People in the room must have heard him because the noise calms down a bit.

The President snaps out of his stupor for a moment. "Okay," he says.

"Mr. President," he begins, "their speed has rendered most of our weapons useless . . . but not all of them."

The crowd hushes a bit more, listening intently for a ray of hope.

"Okay, go on," he says, more interested.

General Hamilton remains standing. "Sir, we have laser detonators. They're kind of like large ray guns," he says, stretching the truth. "These are mounted on humvees and the laser beams travel at the speed of light. The intruders can't out-maneuver lasers. It'll take them down."

"Oh wow!" he says, standing up and feeling more confident now. "That sounds good, General. Let's get those boys going!"

"They're already being deployed, Sir," the general answers then becomes more stoic. "Mr. President, there is another solution."

The room hushes into an eerie silence.

General Hamilton lowers his voice to just above a whisper. "As a last resort, Sir, we can detonate the device once they reach us."

President Harwell remembers. "Ohhh," he whispers. "I'd forgotten about that," he says under his breath. Gritting his teeth he looks down. "Damn," he says. After a few moments he looks up again. "Well let's hope the ray guns do the trick," he says. Smiling and even giving the general a friendly punch on the shoulder. "I don't think this dog's going to bark."

"No, Sir," General Hamilton cautiously says, astonished by the change.

A non-uniformed man comes up to the general and salutes as best he can.

"At ease, Son," the general tells him. "You're not a

soldier."

The non-soldier relaxes. "Yes, Sir," he says.

Only then does he notice the President, he straightens up again. "Mr. President," he says. A medium height, slender, pale and in his mid-twenties: The guy had probably spent most of his life behind a computer screen. "Radar telemetry shows that they are not flying on a direct course."

"That's obvious," General Hamilton says with irritation.

"Yes, Sir," he answers, "But it appears to be flying across large populations while moving in this direction. It slows down to a few hundred miles per hour over these cities and its altitude has never been higher than 3,000 feet."

The general's irritation becomes a restrained anger. "We already knew that!" he bellows. "Why are you even here?!"

The man seems to shrivel. "We don't think they're going to attack."

President Harwell is stunned. "What?" he asks.

The man swallows the lump in his throat. "They fly low and slow over large populations, obviously wanting people to see them. Un-armed people that they could easily destroy. They fly across the entire country rather than drop straight down from space. They're taking the long way around by showing themselves to lots of people, which exposes them to attack. Then they choose to evade those attacks, refusing to engage our fighters. Something's up, Sir. They seem to want everyone to know they're here and that they're coming to see you." He looks at President Harwell.

President Harwell realizes what this means. "Oh crap!" he exclaims, and sits down again.

General Hamilton sighs, and then shoots a look at the pale man. "Dismissed," he says quietly.

The man leaves.

The general sighs again and sits next to the President who is now sitting and hunched over. "Crap!" he keeps saying under his breath. The President looks up at the general. "It's one thing if they're going to destroy all of us. It would be really bad, but at least our suffering will end at some point. But they're after me. **Me!!** Personally! Who knows how long they can . . ." He trails off, wincing at the terrors and tortures his brain has created then jumps back into the conversation. "And they're going to be here in four minutes."

The general seems to want to cheer him up, but remains formal. "I hate to tell you this, Mr. President, but it's two minutes now."

"Oh God!" he cries.

"Mr. President," the general says in a stern whisper, "Get ahold of yourself! The people need you, Sir. Now more than ever before."

Immediately inspired, President Harwell sits up straight. "You're right, Alan." He straightens his tie and stands up. The general also stands. "'The only thing we have to fear is fear itself.'"

"Mr. President," the general says, "he could easily be wrong. Low and slow over large populations could be a psychological attack, terror tactics. They could be saying, 'You have no chance of defeating us.' It might not be friendly aliens."

The President straightens his tie again. "Whether it's a psychological attack or friendly aliens," he says, "this is a diplomatic situation, and I am the President of the United States."

General Hamilton straightens his body, almost standing at attention. "Mr. President," he says, "it is my **duty** to present you with strategic facts and possible courses of action. This is an extremely unusual situation and you need **real** strategic alternatives - not the hopeful stories of Hollywood."

"I understand," he says, "and it's appreciated. But these aliens are exposing themselves and have gone out of their way to prevent a battle, even when we fired first. There's a good chance for a peaceful meeting."

President Harwell changes his tone. Until now, he had been speaking to the general like a friend speaks to another friend. Now he speaks to the general like a boss speaks to an employee.

"Get as many of the laser cannons as you can get. I want them on the White House lawn by the time that thing gets here." He speaks very precisely and very clearly. "**Do not fire** unless I give the order."

"What if you are incapacitated, Mr. President?" the general asks.

He starts to walk out the door and says, "Then I don't care. Do I?" General Hamilton gives him stern look. "Just kidding," the President says. "The vice president can decide what to do."

The white-haired president stops at the doorway, smiles and looks back. "I feel much better now," he admits. "I feel like I just spent a few hours in therapy." He turns and walks out of the room. "They'll be here in less than two minutes, people!" he bellows down the hall. "Let's get ready!"

The general spots the CIA Director, who'd been lurking nearby. "This is all over the news," he says, waving his hand. "There's nothing secret about this," the general tells him, "so why are you here?"

The director leans toward the general. "He's the one that got rid of the other guy, you know," he says, avoiding the question, "Of course he wanted the job!"

The general knows it's probably true, but gets angry, anyway. "Allegedly," he snaps . . . then dutifully follows the President.

Chapter 5
Pidima

The accepted theory about the universe's creation, The Big Bang Theory, not the TV show, began in 1929. It wasn't named until 1949. It's been getting one 'bandage' after ever since, hoping that no one will notice. It states that the entire universe began with a giant explosion . . . a bang. That's why other galaxies are moving away from the Milky Way Galaxy, but that's not entirely true. A few are moving toward it, and a few are colliding with it right now. An explosion doesn't work that way. Another fact is that scientists can't account for ninety-four percent of the universe. They say neutrinos, dark matter, dark energy or something else causes it. All the bandages in the world can't turn a wrong theory into a right one. There are more facts, too.

General Hamilton walks into the Situation Room to find the President looking at digital footage on a 20-foot video screen, following the giant ship's movements. A red line connects the cities that are highlighted with red circles. The general walks across the room and stands next to the President in front of the huge screen. The line connects Los Angeles to Las Vegas to Denver to Lincoln to Chicago to Cleveland to Pittsburgh. Washington D.C. has two red circles. Green circles highlight Detroit, Indianapolis, Columbus, Cincinnati, Philadelphia, Baltimore, Boston and New York City.

"They've paused over Pittsburgh," the President says to the general. "That gives us a little more time."

The general already realizes that. "Yes, Mr. President," he says anyway.

President Harwell continues. "I figure that this is as good a place as any to wait for the inevitable."

General Hamilton takes a deep breath. "That's true, Sir," he says. "We can watch its movements very well in here."

The President turns to face a third person in the room. "Zoom in," he tells a tech. It's the same pale man from earlier: short brown hair, blue eyes and slender. The huge screen immediately zooms to show a 300-mile radius around Washington, D.C. Seconds later an arrowed red line begins to move again, rocketing toward Washington.

"Damn, it's fast," President Harwell tells the general. "That trip is nearly an hour by air."

"Yes, Sir," the general replies. "They are moving about 5,000 miles per hour. Only the *Aurora* can match that speed."

President Harwell turns his head and looks at him. "The what?" he asks.

The general's face becomes blank and rigid. "Nothing, Mr. President," he says. He still feels the President's stare on the side of his face. "I was talking about the Aurora Borealis, Mr. President."

President Harwell turns back to the screen, chuckling. "You military guys have a strange way of looking at the world."

General Hamilton chuckles aloud while silently breathing a sigh of relief. *This president is a breeze*, he thinks to himself. *Either of the two Bushes, or God forbid, Reagan, would have definitely gotten it out of me.*

The President looks at the tech. The tech doesn't wear glasses, but his pale face seems to glow behind the computer screen. "What do you expect they'll do once they arrive, Mr. Asher?" President Harwell asks him.

The tech looks up for a moment, unsure that he'd heard his name at all. He sees the President's gaze and immediately becomes excited. *The President of the United States knows my name!* he excitedly thinks. He tries to keep his excitement in check, but a slight grin escapes, anyway.

Asher wipes the grin off his face as fast as he can, and speaks with all the authority he can muster. "They'll probably hover overhead for several hours," the young man answers. Feeling a bit more certain, he continues. "That's a really, really big ship, so they'll need to send down a shuttle."

The general discretely clears his throat, signaling the tech.

"Mr. President," Asher hastily adds.

Pleased by the news, President Harwell smiles. "We have

more time than we thought!" he says.

Asher almost says something, but General Hamilton puts a finger to his lips, signaling for Asher to be silent.

"I'm starving," the President says. "Who's up for pasta? I'll have the kitchen make some," he says as he walks out of the room.

General Hamilton dutifully follows him again. "Not a word to anyone," he quietly tells Asher as he walks out of the room.

"Yes, Sir," Asher says quietly.

Alone in the room and alone with his thoughts, replaying the last few minutes in his mind, Asher kicks himself. *Joseph Harwell is the President of the United States of America,* he thinks, *and NOT one of my buddies. He deserves more respect than I am giving him. He's the most powerful man on the planet, or at least he WAS. I need to make a much stronger effort.*

In the Streets of Washington, D.C.

A vast and mysterious shadow silently crosses the Capital City. A dusk-like twilight covers dozens upon dozens of city blocks in every direction as the massive ship's partial-shadow engulfs them, bringing streetlights to life. Seconds later the midnight-black umbra reaches them. Sunlit streets turn into inky black coffins in mere seconds.

Confusion becomes panic. Sheer panic. People realize the alien ship is not just passing by, it's coming **here**. They scream unnaturally and shout profanities at the top of their lungs. Panicked birds screech profanities of their own, but the enormous ship makes no sound at all . . . even at only six hundred feet in the air. Car horns blare, tires squeal and metal smashes into metal.

A mother pushing a stroller suddenly stops and covers the slumbering infant. "Oh, my God!" she screams. "My baby! Help my baby!"

News journalists broadcast the event while the leviathan finally comes to a halt directly above the White House. Visions of disaster, **major** disaster, pound the minds of millions of people.

President Harwell watches the event on his massive video screen then runs to a window. "My God!" he yells. "It's even bigger than I'd imagined. It's one thing to hear the numbers. It's another thing to see it for yourself."

Stretching from the Grand Hyatt to George Washington University to the Tidal Basin, the monstrous machine hovers over the entire, sprawling city, hanging barely above the top of the Washington Monument. President Harwell turns back to the video screen in time to see a tiny craft launch from the giant ship. Silver and cylindrical, the tiny ship seems to float down to the South Lawn.

The President turns to Asher. "Can't they beam down or something?" he asks.

The pale man proudly answers. "Mr. President, that's the shuttle I mentioned." He feels more of an authority than he did a few moments before. "Sir, beaming is more of a 'TV & movie magic thing' than something real. There's been quite a bit of research on that subject, Sir, but. . ."

President Harwell cuts him off. "You also mentioned that they'd hover for hours," he scolds Asher. "They're hovering alright. Hovering a shuttle to our doorstep! I'd say you're only right half the time!" Filled with testosterone and adrenaline, he turns to the general. "General, are those laser blaster things in place?"

"Yes, Mr. President," General Hamilton says. "On your order."

Alarmed, Asher defends himself. "Mr. President," he asserts, "it's only one out of three times."

President Harwell didn't realize Asher was still there.

"What?" he asks absently.

"If they were hostile, then why did they send only **one** shuttle?" he points out.

The President and the general stop and listen for a few seconds.

"If they're friendly then there'd be no reason to wait. It's likely that the shuttle has very important people on board . . . possibly the most important people they have."

General Hamilton questions Asher's logic. "Why would they send their leader on a recon mission?" he asks.

Asher answers him as plainly as he can. "It's not recon, Sir," he tells him and then explains, "If it's a 'friendly situation,' there's no need for recon." Asher has never felt so alive! His opinions are altering the course of an entire nation, perhaps the whole planet. "Look above you, Sir," he tells the general in a quiet voice. "They have the equivalent of a fleet of warships surrounding us. How much more safe could their leader be?"

The general becomes stoic. "It could **still** be a psychological attack, Mr. President," he says quietly. He turns to face the President, and straightens his uniform. "But Asher's right in that we shouldn't fire on the shuttle. I still recommend that we keep the other option in mind, Mr.

President." The general discretely points down.

President Harwell doesn't seem to understand at first. "Oh yeah!" he suddenly announces in a room filled with people. "You mean the b . . ."

The general shoots an imploring look at him.

The President stops talking and looks around. "Device," he whispers.

Just as their strained nerves start to relax, the same soldier runs up to General Hamilton, and salutes. "They're landing now, Sir. South Lawn."

"Thank you, Son," the general acknowledges. He salutes the young soldier, and dismisses him. As the young man quickly walks away, the general turns to the President. "Mr. President," he says, "I think we should get you into the room the Secret Service designed for you."

President Harwell looks at him in disbelief. "What?" he asks. "And you actually think that'll work? Do you think that would prevent an armada of aliens from finding me and vaporizing me?"

The general tries to correct himself. "Mr. President, I only meant . . ."

The President cuts him off. "Don't worry about it, Alan,"

he says. "Nerves are short right now."

Asher jumps in. "Mr. President," he says, "I think it'd be a significant gesture for you to walk out there to meet them."

Both the general and the President look at him like he's crazy. "You have **got** to be kidding," the general tells him. "Son, we've tolerated . . ."

Asher cuts him off. "Mr. President," he says, looking at the general's reaction for a split second. "There is an alien armada above our heads and possibly their leaders in our backyard. We are beaten. The best course of action is diplomacy."

General Hamilton sighs loudly, and purses him lips. "I hate to admit it, Mr. President," he says, "but Mr. Asher makes a good point." He straightens up. "Diplomacy is always a good option and . . . as much as I hate to admit it, we have been beaten," he says, mumbling the last words.

Asher thinks the general is accepting defeat too easily, and he probably has a trick up his sleeve.

The general continues. "I **really** don't like the idea of you walking out there by yourself, Mr. President, but I'd consider it an honor if I walked out there with you."

President Harwell smiles. "I expected that you would," he

says.

People step aside as the two men walk out the back part of the White House. The general opens a door to the South Lawn, and sees the silver craft about 100 yards in front of them, hovering a couple of feet above the manicured grass. One or two people cling to the porch, but the area is otherwise devoid of them.

What began as a clear and sunny day, now feels dark, strangely windy and icy cold. As if the massive alien ship heard their thoughts, colossal lights under the massive ship ignite, bathing the entire South Lawn in daylight.

General Hamilton smiles. "I guess they know you're here," he says.

He can now see that the silver craft is a simple seven-foot tall metal cylinder. He thought the ends were flat at first, but can now see that the ends are slightly rounded. Looking like a giant soda can, minus the paint, the mysterious ship is only 15 feet long with no windows at all.

The two men walk carefully toward the silver craft. Each footstep is a footstep into the unknown, and tension builds with each one.

President Harwell's eyes refuse to blink, and he has to keep reminding himself to unclench his hands.

About 20 yards away, there's a hissing sound.

Both men stop dead in their tracks.

A portion of the silver craft's hull seems to melt away, leaving a perfectly shaped doorway. The molten metal sinks into invisible molds, forming steps that hover in mid-air.

President Harwell's pulse seems to stop as a foot emerges, landing on the newly formed stairs.

Chapter 6
The Others

With the wind slowly blowing in a large circle around the continent and located ENTIRELY within the Antarctic Circle, Antarctica is much colder than its northern counterpart. Only a few animals and some lichen can call it 'home,' making Antarctica the most lifeless continent on Earth. Barren, nearly lifeless, no active geology, eternally frigid: and yet a mystery remains. Most of the ice is less than 13,000 years old. Why is that? Shouldn't it be millions of years old? What happened 13,000 years ago?

The foot becomes a leg, and the leg becomes a man . . . a human man, descending from the silver craft's steps.

The President and the general relax a little.

The white male human-alien has shoulder-length blond hair, and wears a loose-fitting white garment with long sleeves. The garment has snug-fitting red 'cuffs' around his neck, wrists and ankles. He wears a red cummerbund around his waist.

Holding a dark brown spear-like device about five feet long in his right hand, the human-alien man steps down and onto the grass, but remains expressionless as he stands near the stairs.

The general wonders about the weapon.

Green eyes stare blankly at the two men.

Suddenly another foot appears from the craft. The first man seems to come to attention as an older man appears from the craft. He has gray hair and a nearly-trimmed gray beard, wearing a light gray garment that looks something like a suit. It has a gray vest and a red cummerbund with dangling tips.

The second man immediately approaches the President, stops and bows his head slightly. "Greetings from Atlantis!" he says with a deep baritone voice.

Completely and totally stunned, the President immediately turns to his diplomatic etiquette. "I am President Joseph R. Harwell and this is General Alan Hamilton, my Joint Chiefs of Staff Chairman. We are pleased to meet you." He carefully extends his hand.

The bearded man looks at the President's hand for a moment then grasps it. "We are also pleased to meet you," he says. "I am G'brael, leader of the Atlantean people and this is S'lon, my guard and assistant."

S'lon nods, but doesn't divulge any emotion at all.

"We have been waiting for this opportunity for many, many years."

President Harwell relaxes a bit more. "We've heard of Atlantis, but I never took it to be anything more than a myth," he says.

"The island of Atlantis sank long ago," G'brael replies, "and the underwater city built later has the same name."

General Hamilton is genuinely interested. "Admittedly," he says, "I have a strong interest in our culture's old legends. I always thought the two cities were the same thing."

G'brael smiles. "Not at all," he says. "'Atlantis' is the name of the first human city built underwater. We named it the same thing as our old city, as a symbol. Irish cultures called us 'Hy-Brasil, which refers to us as 'descendants.' That's true, actually."

"My ship," G'brael continues, "is a light brown color. It looks like and island or the horn of a continent when it emerges from the ocean, so the old Irish thought it was invisible most of the time. Over time, the name became synonymous with 'underwater city,' but seven more cities were built . . . and none of them are called 'Atlantis,' either." He smiles again, like he just made a joke.

General Hamilton's mouth hangs open. "Eight cities?" he manages. "Alien cities on Earth?"

G'brael nearly laughs. "They're not aliens," he says. "They're Lemurians, the first sentient species to evolve on Earth!" He looks above and behind him. "And here they come!"

The President and the general look up, both surprised and apprehensive. A second silver craft, identical to the first, quietly makes its final approach to the President's left. Neither man had noticed it before now.

"Such stealth is frightening," General Hamilton tells the President in a low voice as the silver craft comes to rest, just above the grass.

The President nods in agreement. The technology in front of them is far more advanced than anything America has ever produced.

G'brael turns his gaze away from the second craft, and to the President. "Lemurians built the first two underwater cities," he tells them. "My people have worked closely with their people since the ocean swallowed our first city nearly 10,000 years ago. I'm pretty sure you're safe." He smiles coyly, like he made another joke, before turning his gaze back to the second craft.

The silver vessel lands, hovering a couple of feet above the grass. The door melts away to form steps, just like the first craft did.

The President unconsciously holds his breath.

A small foot steps onto the newly formed stairs.

The general maintains a solid look on the exterior, but his heart is beating so hard that it feels like it will rip straight through his chest.

The foot becomes a leg and the leg becomes a short, grayish alien with big, black eyes. Another immediately follows him . . . or is it a her?

Only 3 ½ feet tall, both creatures are dressed in dark gray, slick-looking uniforms, like some sort of jumpsuit. Their skin is light gray, but still gray . . . and those eyes! Those big, solid black eyes! They stick out like an ant's head . . . a giant ant's head. Those gray aliens don't even have a nose! Just four grooves where a nose should be. They don't have antenna, six legs or clamping jaws, but they look like some kind of ant people.

One of the gray creatures walks up to President Harwell, who is completely stunned with fear.

Turning to G'brael, one of the Lemurians says something that sounds like a bass guitar playing Morse Code.

"Yes," G'brael replies. "They've come alone. Our sensors prove it."

The small creature turns to face the President. "President Harwell," G'brael says, "this is a Lemurian . . . 'Wah-wah'."

The President and the general fight the urge to snicker. "I'm sorry," President Harwell says. "Did you say his name is 'Wawa'?"

Lemurian

G'brael knows about the old Saturday Night Live sketch,

and sighs melodramatically. "Yes, I did," he replies. "W-A-H-W-A-H. The other one's name is 'Pahp'. P-A-H-P."

This time, the President and the general fight the urge to burst out laughing.

"How did you understand him?" the President asks, with obvious effort.

"I can understand any language," he replies. "Even gibberish. I'll spare you the details, but I have a ring implanted around my brain that allows me to sense what the person intends to say, which bypasses the language used. It's in a different part of the brain from language. Actually, it's several areas of the brain."

He traces his fingers from the very top of his head and to the back, near his neck. "The ring is a tilted, circular antenna that faces forward when I look at someone," he tells them. "It tells my brain what a person means to say. It also controls my tongue and lips to reproduce the same language in return, while building up a database of that language. I know English anyway, but I would speak Portuguese if **you** spoke Portuguese. The same would be true for any other language."

"Why don't you just wear the ring on your finger?" President Harwell asks. "That would keep you away from major surgery."

G'brael fights the urge to snicker this time. "It's not that kind of ring," he says. "And there's no surgery involved. We use a series of injections that become solid once they are inside the body." He moves his fingers around his head again. "This type of ring is much larger, and encircles my whole brain. It does quite a bit more than translation. We used to wear them on the outside of our heads, and even gave one to King Solomon of Israel."

Asher has been watching on a video monitor. G'brael has been dropping lots of highly valuable pieces of information, clues to Mankind's past.

"People called it 'The Ring of Solomon' back then," G'brael continues, "but I think your people call it something else now. You might need one when you meet other species."

President Harwell's stomach knots for the **hundredth** time today.

"Lemurians were the first sentient species on Earth," G'brael continues. "They emerged from the Arthropods nearly 500 million years ago and reached sentience 300 million years ago. They don't have tongues, so they can't speak English or any other human language. Human cultures, as different as they seem to be, are remarkably similar. You'll see what I mean when you meet some of the Foreign

Nationals."

"What did you say?" an apprehensive President Harwell asks. "Genuine aliens?"

G'brael explains. "They are alien to your world" he says. "But not much more than a Japanese man is alien to the United States of America. This type of person eats, sleeps, breathes air, is born and dies; just like any one of your citizens. They are Foreign Nationals, and don't live here. They trade with us like you do with Japan."

Feeling a little more secure now. "Are they slimy and telepathic with tentacles?" he curiously asks.

G'brael laughs again. "Not at all," he says. "No creature can operate electrical equipment if it's slimy. It will electrocute itself and short out the circuit in the process! What you perceive as telepathy is actually radio. Some robots are built so that it looks like a human, or the species of its builder. That's called an android. S'lon is one of those androids."

The President and the general look over at S'lon, but he simply nods again. They stare at him intently, but still can't tell that he's not human.

G'brael continues. "Androids signal each other with radio," he says, "like two people talking on walkie-talkies. As for the tentacles: It's true that some aliens have them, but they are all animals that live on an alien's home planet, like the octopus lives here on Earth. Tentacles are can have enormous amounts of strength as well as incredibly fine manipulation, but it just doesn't happen out there. Most sentient creatures have two arms, two legs, one head and stand upright. Those characteristics are the most effective for developing high enough levels of technology."

Inside the White House

General Hamilton escorts President Harwell, the two human-aliens and the two Lemurians into the main conference room inside the White House. Several dignitaries sit around a large and ornate conference table.

Asher sits among them. He is the main technical advisor, but more importantly, he is something of an expert on Atlantean thinking.

General Hamilton opens the door and everyone stands.

President Harwell walks into the room, stands behind a podium and announces to the room. "Please stand up . . . I mean continue standing for four men . . . creatures . . . I mean visitors. They come to us from the underwater city of Atlantis. Please help me welcome G'brael, S'lon and our small friends, the Lemurians. We know them as the Grays."

The President and everyone politely clap as the two humans enter the room. The clapping slows and softens as the two Lemurians enter the room. People that are closest to the door back away a little.

The Lemurians climb into chairs at the conference table like a small child would do it. Their legs barely reach the end of the chairs' seats, and their chins don't quite reach over the table. Their black eyes, nearly on top of their large heads, make them look like frogs sticking their heads out of the water. Although they are only the size of small human children, several people standing close to them slowly back away.

When most of the clapping had stopped, G'brael leans to President Harwell's ear. "Lemurians are not Grays," he whispers.

President Harwell looks up at him, confused. "But they're gray," he says. "They have big heads and black eyes."

G'brael smiles. "There are **several** species of gray aliens in the galaxy," he says. "That's like saying a Mexican man and an Egyptian man were the same since they both have brown skin and brown eyes." He pats the President on the shoulder. "You'll see what I mean when you meet the Foreign Nationals."

G'brael starts to move to the podium, but President Harwell stops him and nervously asks. "How . . . how many more are there?"

G'brael pauses. "We trade with 23 planets," he says. "As for how many more are out there," smiling devilishly, "that's for you to find out for yourself." He smiles and pats the President on the shoulder before walking away.

G'brael stands behind the podium and addresses the room. "I have an announcement!"

Reticulan (Gray)

The room isn't loud, but grows quieter anyway.

"There is a reason we flew over some of your most populated cities the way we did. There is a reason why we refused to fire at your open hostility. You have grown out of your adolescence and there won't be any more secrets. Video of this meeting is being broadcast around the world as we speak, and interruption of alien communications is stopping right now. This is the fifth and final Era of Mankind. You are one of us . . . and we were the gods of your ancient world. You are more advanced and more powerful than you realize. A new chapter in Human History begins today, and it is time to take your place in the galaxy."

He starts to walk away from the podium, but stops. "The biggest secret will be the most difficult for you to believe," he says. "I know that serpents have drilled and drilled the opposite thought into your heads, but . . . **<u>Humans aren't stupid!</u>**" He emphasizes each word and pauses for a few moments, allowing the words to sink in.

"In fact," he continues, "humans are the smartest life forms in the entire galaxy." Again, he waits for his words to sink into people.

"Many of you might think that this doesn't apply to you, but you'd be wrong. Earth is the MIT of the entire galaxy! Just make it through elementary school here and you've beaten 99% of the galaxy."

"Think about it like this," he explains. "A computer built in 1950 versus one built in 2020. The 1950 model is far, far slower, but has been doing things for **<u>seventy years</u>**. It's technology designed the SR-71 Blackbird aircraft, ran the

Apollo missions to the moon and was the basis for every computer built after it. The 2020 model is much faster, but hasn't had time to accomplish much. It doesn't need the extra time, though, because it's almost caught up to the old computers!"

G'brael explains. "Lemurians gained sentience 300 **million** years ago," he tells them. "Humans gained it only 100 **thousand** years ago, so to speak, and haven't had time to accomplish nearly as much, but that doesn't matter. You are the latest models of sentient life forms in the galaxy. You don't need extra time, because you've **already** almost caught up!"

A few people grasp the gravity of what he is telling them, but only a few.

G'brael speaks softly for a few moments. "You are so close . . . so very close . . . and you don't even realize it. One of your brethren once said that any sufficiently advanced technology is indistinguishable from magic. Four hundred years ago, how many things were explained by calling it 'magic'? How about 100 years ago? How about today?"

His words create a stir in the room. "When you go see a magician, do you say, 'He's really magic!' or do you ask, 'How did he do that?'"

The people mumble to each other.

"Wouldn't that mean that you are so advanced that **nothing** is considered 'magic' anymore?"

He smiles, like a proud father smiles at his child. "That doesn't mean things aren't beautiful or special. That just means you don't use the word 'magic' to explain the unknown anymore. You are almost grown up now. Technology is merely a convenience. Nothing more. It's much more important to organize yourselves well. Fundamentals are not very exciting, but they are quite powerful. You are a collection of individual people, not a collection of interchangeable parts. Remember that. The sheer power of an individual is astounding. You will truly impress yourselves with your own ingenuity. Communism and socialism are merely survival techniques. If they are used on a large scale for more than a few years, they destroy individuals. Not all at once and definitely not instantly. Leaders can only speed it up or slow down the process. They're not the real problem . . . bureaucracies are. Don't get me wrong. Some bureaucracy is necessary, but it needs **far** more size-management than anything else does. Most of them need to be downsized out of existence. Reduce bureaucracies to an absolute minimum then cut them in **half**. Your Founding Fathers gave you only three Cabinet positions for a reason. Only after you do those things will you begin to taste freedom again."

G'brael continues. "We built a few stone monuments for navigation, but **you** built all the other amazing monuments on this planet . . . all by yourselves. Serpents will try to convince you otherwise, but 'No.' You did them yourselves. Self-reliance is your most powerful ally, but a good teacher needs to impart a few fundamentals every now and then. There **is** a God. We have physical proof. You have that proof, too. You just don't realize it. You were **never** Neanderthals. You are our children. No matter how much you try to contain it, Socialism will always turn into Communism, and it kills **far** more people than it saves. There was **no** Big Bang. The universe is a lot bigger and a lot older than you think it is. There is **no** Higgs Boson. There are **eleven** dimensions of space-time, not three or four . . . and they are all, quite literally, in the palm of your hand."

Many people look at their hands.

G'brael continues speaking. "False beliefs like these and others have impeded your people for more than a century. You have a century's worth of wisdom. Believe it not. Fundamentals may not be exciting, but they **are** the answer. Remember that and you will make up that century in a decade. You once called us gods then you called us angels. Now we want you to call us friends. You are our sons and daughters . . . and you are more clever than any other Era of Mankind has ever been. We will see you again in **our** home. Until then, we bid you a very fond farewell." With that, G'brael steps away from the podium.

Some people applaud while others shout: "What?," "Where are you going?," and "But we need you." The people applauding G'brael stare at those shouting. They drown them out with applause in a standing ovation.

G'brael tries to walk past President Harwell and toward the exit, but the President grabs his arm.

"Where are you going?" President Harwell asks.

G'brael stops. "We are going home," he tells him.

"Have we offended you in some way?" President Harwell asks.

"You haven't offended us at all," G'brael replies. "In fact, you've beaten every other Era of Mankind by more than two and a half millennia. That's why we didn't stop you from spreading across the entire globe. We couldn't be more pleased with you."

President Harwell looks like a child begging a parent. "But we need you," he pleads.

G'brael looks at him and smiles. "You need us as much today as you did yesterday." He gives him a friendly pat on the shoulder. "Remember what I've said," he tells him. "I have complete faith in your people." He reaches for the door handle, but the door opens from the other side.

A beautiful red-haired woman walks through it. "Maybe they don't want to jump through your hoops, G'brael," she says.

G'brael's eyes show his shock. "L'lith!" he gasps, immediately turns his eyes away from hers.

The Lemurians look up in horror.

"It is not your place to come here, L'lith," he tells her, growing more and more angry. "You were never invited."

Wearing an ankle-length black skirt, a black bodice and black cape with blue, leather pauldrons, she smiles coyly and seems to glide into the room. "You forgot to invite me, G'brael," she says. "One might think that you didn't want the Americans to know there were other opinions out there."

G'brael's face grows red, but manages to keep his voice under control. "That's not it, L'lith." Gritting his teeth he adds, "and you know it."

When L'lith moves toward the conference table, the

Lemurians slide off the chairs and run for the open door.

"I never liked them anyway," she mutters.

She turns around and leans against the conference table. Her cape is black on the outside, but blue on the inside. Her skirt parts in the front, revealing the blue underside, just like her cape. Long, black leather boots complete her sleek wardrobe.

"I am L'lith," she announces to the room, "leader of the Osirian City-State. It's one of ten city-states built under Earth's oceans."

G'brael breaks in. "There are two Lemurian city-states," he clarifies for the room, "and one city-state doesn't exist anymore."

She ignores him. "From an **unbiased** perspective," she says, "I see you swooping in here, dangling your toys in front of their faces and then leaving. Where have I gotten it wrong?"

"I wasn't dangling anything," he says. "I told them who they are, and gave them clues . . ."

L'lith immediately cuts him off. "Clues?" she implores. "Clues?! For crying out loud, G'brael, these are your **children**! Give them more than just clues! You're a teacher. Give them a spaceship, and **teach** them how it works. Teach them how to manipulate gravity. Teach them how Faster-Than-Light travel works. Teach them **something**."

G'brael's face isn't as red as it was earlier, but he is still consciously controlling the volume of his voice. "This is a very old argument, L'lith," he says. "I've already given them the clues they need to solve those puzzles and others. Emotional motivations might help in the short run, but they can do serious damage in the long run. I've seen it myself."

L'lith pretends to ponder. "Hmm," she says, brushing her chin with the back of her hand. "And since women are more emotionally motivated than men . . ." She pauses for a few moments, for dramatic effect. "Is that why you don't let women vote in Atlantis?"

G'brael is immediately enraged. "That's a bold-faced lie, L'lith! All of our women have the right to vote and some do it. Some women even hold office, but many **choose** not to participate."

"Jim Crow Laws," she says under her breath. "Let me guess," she counters. "Some actions reduce estrogen and politics is one of them."

He shakes his head. "No," he corrects her. "It increases **testosterone**. The aggression and competition needed for those things, increases the **ratio** of testosterone to estrogen.

Both genders make both hormones, but estrogen is significantly greater in women while testosterone is significantly greater in men. A woman's behavior reduces the **ratio** of estrogen to testosterone and makes them more masculine. Your method makes them look like men. They'll even wear pantsuits! That's why they won't do it."

She balks. "Women don't **have** testosterone," she tells him.

Exasperated, he sighs. "Then why do women take 'hormone replacement pills' after menopause?" he asks. "People make many different choices for many different reasons, not the same choice for the same reason. Voting is a choice . . . not a mandate. People are individuals, not cattle."

She looks at him for a moment. "Moo," she mimics. "Clever rationalization, G'brael," she tells him. "You're not going to help the Americans. Are you?"

"We already did," he says. "We took away road-blocks and gave them the clues they need to solve everything for themselves."

L'lith looks at the ground and shakes her head. "It's a real tragedy when parents refuse to be parents," she says. She turns around, and announces to the room again. "The Osirian people will help you. We'll teach you about gravity, Faster-Than-

Light technology and even alien life."

Excitement fills the room like oxygen, filling each person with desire. Many people cheer, and others chant, "Osiria! Osiria! Osiria!"

An enormous man, at least seven feet tall, enters the room. Heavily muscled, he wears black battle armor and a cape that reaches the floor. It has the same black overside with blue underside colors as L'lith's cape. He has short-cropped hair and a pointed goatee.

Gasping at the sight of him, the people fall silent.

"P'al!" G'brael says, astonished.

"**General** P'al," L'lith corrects him. "You have your First, Harwell has his and so do I." She turns to Harwell, "This is General P'al, Supreme Commander of the Cherubim."

G'brael calmly leans toward President Harwell. "The Osirian army." he tells him.

General Hamilton notices the six silver stars on his collar: five in the shape of a pentagon and one in the middle.

L'lith is annoyed. "G'brael, shouldn't you be leaving?" she asks.

G'brael fakes a smile. "Time to go, S'lon," he says loudly, then whispers to President Harwell. "This will be the greatest

test Mankind has ever known. Choose wisely."

President Harwell looks imploringly at him.

G'brael starts to walk out the door. "I know you will," he tells the President, patting him on the shoulder again.

Having lost the crowd at the eleventh hour, G'brael and S'lon can do nothing more than to silently walk out of the room.

Chapter 7
There Be Dragons!

The Ancient Greek sophist Flavius Philostratus wrote of three types of dragons infesting ancient India. Many of his reports sound like 'men' operating machines. "It emits a fire brighter than any torch," "a burrowing dragon sounds like clashing brass," "there are colorful gems in a dragon's head" and so on. Other parts of his reports do not, though. "Dragons enjoy swimming" and "their hearts, livers and meat are edible." He never mentions breathing fire or flying, but noted that the Greek poet Homer described them better than other poets. More descriptions? Is this lost knowledge? Are these descriptions about non-human individuals operating machinery?

Ten years later, Dr. Livingston is hovering over his computer screen in the same office, when Richard walks in. "Richard," he says, "you won't believe the data the satellites got today. It's amazing! Staggering stuff!"

Richard calmly stands in front of Bill's desk. "**Bill**," he says quietly, "you didn't see the news this morning. Did you?"

Bill's glasses reflect the computer screen while he works, but spares a moment's glance at Richard before looking back to his precious computer. "I don't watch TV very often," he says. "It's all about bad news, worse news and even worse news."

Richard sighs and calmly sits on the corner of Bill's desk. "Well," he tells Bill, "I have a feeling they'll be banging on your door before the day is out."

Bill stops what he's doing on the computer, and looks at his face. "Richard," he objects, "this stuff is amazing, yes, but it still has to be verified by several sources. It'll take some time. By the end of the week, maybe, but . . ."

Richard hops off of the desk. "Bill," he asserts, "aliens landed on the White House lawn this morning!"

Stunned. "What?" Bill asks, as if he has just woken up from a dream.

Richard yells again. *"Close Encounters, E.T.,* 'They're here!'" he shouts. "It all went down this morning!"

Bill looks amused. "That was *Poltergeist,*" he says. "Ghosts, not aliens." He sits back in his chair. "You know I've thought about that. Personally I think there are several species of aliens."

"We know that, too, Bill," he says.

Bill sits forward in his chair. "You saw the dragons?" he asks.

Richard is stunned for a moment and looks at him blankly. "I didn't see any dragons, Bill," he says, "There were human-aliens and a couple of gray alien-things."

Bill immediately closes the files on his computer screen and opens new ones. "The human-aliens weren't aliens at all," he says. "They are an older version of Earth-humans. Here is the ancient Greek word for 'dragon' and here's the one for 'serpent.'"

Richard walks around the desk and looks at the screen. "They aren't spelled alike," Bill explains, "but they are **pronounced** like each other. Remember that most people at this time are illiterate."

"In Europe," he continues, "dragons can fly, but when they're in Asia, they can only walk. They breathe fire on both continents. A snake slithers. They knew that. That's a totally different word. They weren't talking about snakes."

Bill opens file after file on his computer. "Finnish, Norse, Celtic, Germanic, Polish, French and Macedonian legends all talk about flying, fire-breathing dragons. Some even have historical accounts." Richard doubted everything so far, but he knew better than to interrupt Bill when he got going with something.

"Mayan, Aztec, Egyptian, Sumerian, Persian, Chinese, Japanese and Korean legends talk of a flying serpent that did **not** breathe fire. Christian, Chinese, Korean, Jewish and Islamic mythologies talk of a reptile, usually calling it a serpent, which would **walk** and even **speak**. I can go on and on. I think all these cultures were talking about the **same**

thing."

Richard stops him. "Wait a minute, Bill!" he says. "How are these anything like each other? Humans are hard-wired to think of reptiles as dangerous creatures. It's probably something left over from evolution." Richard sometimes unconsciously gives Bill hints about his true intelligence.

Bill smiles for a moment. "A sentient reptile in a fighter jet," he says confidently.

Richard bursts out laughing. "Oh, come on, Bill!" he manages. "You've gone off the deep end on this one! Ooh!" he says, waving his hands around. He pretends to whisper a secret. "I heard that Bigfoot is behind a lot of this stuff. He's an alien, you know."

Bill just rolls his eyes and quietly takes the ridicule. He's used to it. After a few minutes, Richard runs out of jokes and Bill starts to work on him. "Think of it scientifically," he says.

Richard stops laughing and listens, but maintains his smirk. "Okay," he says.

"All these cultures have dragon legends," Bill starts. "One possible explanation is an evolutionary fear of reptiles. Some cultures emphasize that fear more than others."

Richard nods. "That's right," he says.

Bill continues. "I suggest that dragons are an intelligent species of reptiles using fighter jets."

Richard snickers, but manages not to say anything.

"A creature with wings is just a metaphor for a creature that **can** fly, either naturally or mechanically. The word 'serpent' is another word for 'reptile.' Something that 'breathes fire' is yet another metaphor for 'cause fire from a distance.'"

Richard stops snickering and stares intently at Bill's computer screen.

"Hindu mythology talks about Garuda, a bird-like creature, the mount of the god Vishnu and sworn enemy of the Naga serpent race. Polish records mention the *olophagus* Smok. They don't call it a dragon. Other people do. You know what *olophagus* means. Don't you?"

Richard can see the writing on the wall, and closes his eyes. "Swallows whole," he quietly admits.

"A bird and reptile trait," Bill says, beaming with delight. "'Homer's City of Troy' was thought to be a story . . . until Heinrich Schliemann uncovered it in 1868. Homer intuitively described the feet of male versus female crayfish. Only recently have people realized that he was right. He also described the red back of a marsh dragon. People even say

Grendel was a walking dragon."

Richard opens his eyes. "From <u>Beowulf</u>?" he asks.

"Yep," Bill excitedly answers. "Grendel can rip men apart to swallow them, and even a razor-sharp sword can't penetrate his skin. Sound familiar? Beowulf grabbed Grendel by the hand . . . and you know the rest. I always wondered why Beowulf could grab Grendel by the hand and not have his own arm ripped off. Grendel can rip a man apart, but his arms can't do it."

Richard is genuinely interested now. "So if he doesn't use his hands, then how does he rip the man apart?"

Bill grabs an apple off his desk, sinks his teeth into it and then turns his head to rip a chunk out of it.

Richard gasps. "I see!" he says. "Why doesn't he bite Beowulf, then?"

Livingston has been waiting for this question. "I think he tried," Bill answers. "Maybe several times, but since Beowulf has Grendel by the hand, he keeps putting Grendel's arm between himself and Grendel's teeth. I think Grendel bit his own arm by accident, and Beowulf cut off the rest of the arm."

Richard nods in agreement. "Okay," he acknowledges. "You and I both know that there's no such thing as 'impenetrable.' Anything can be penetrated, and Grendel's skin would be no different. A human wielding a sword might not be able to do it, but I can see how the teeth and jaw muscles of a dragon could do it. Bite strength is what led people to realize that the 18th Century's Beast of Gévaudan was a serial killer using a hyena, and not a werewolf."

Bill likes this type of thing. Two scholars talking, and making references to vastly different subjects. *They're more related than most people realize,* he thinks.

"You know," Bill tells him, "*T. rex's* arms were tiny compared to his body, but they were only slightly larger than human arms. In an arm-wrestling match, the *T. rex* has the strength to win, but he couldn't rotate his arm enough to finish the match. The story says that Grendel pulled his arm too close, and Beowulf used a sword to cut off the arm. Beowulf doesn't have enormous strength. He has a good understanding of Grendel's skeletal structure . . . and he has experience."

Richard scoffs. "Eighth century England is nowhere near the Cretaceous Period!" he says.

Bill calmly counters. "Not a tyrannosaur," he replies, "but something with a similar skeleton. A reptile with a bird's skeleton, a Theropod. Believe it or not, *T. rex* was the 4th smartest of **all** the dinosaurs."

Richard gasps. "You're kidding me?" he asks. "Right?" He looks for a glimmer of humor in Bill's eyes, but doesn't see any. "I've always thought of *T. rex* as a big, dumb brute!" he says.

Bill retorts. "Brute, yes. Dumb, no." Bill laughs to himself. "At least in the world of **dinosaurs**, he was smart. Most dinosaurs were just big, dumb lizards . . . but things were changing. All of the top 10 smartest dinosaurs were Theropods! They say that *Troodon* was the smartest dinosaur, but I think it was Velociraptor, which they call #2. *Troodon* was about a foot taller than *Velociraptor*. That'd be like saying that a 6'6&" person is smarter than a 5'6" person, just because his brain is larger."

He continues. "*Velociraptor* would be a good candidate for the dragon," he says. "That type of dinosaur was an evolutionary leap forward. It was almost five times smarter than the next smartest dinosaur. Paleontologists look at the imprint of their brains on the inside of their skulls."

Richard shakes his head. "I don't know," he says. "I'm with you on the dinosaurs, but your theory about dragons sounds flimsy to me, but I also know your theories have a habit of coming true."

He opens other computer files, like he's trying to defend

his theory. "I have more than that," Bill replies. "Much more."

"It's okay, Bill," he says. "I know better than to doubt you."

Bill looks relieved. "Going back to our original conversation," he says, "at this thing at the White House with the aliens. Were there any misshapen humans?"

Richard blankly looks at Bill then gasps. "Now that you mention it, there was one guy that was really, really tall and muscular," he says. "He also talked funny."

Bill points with his finger. "That's him," he says. "That's the dragon. There were two different species of *Velociraptor*. We know a lot about one of them, but we don't know much about the other. He's hiding his true form." Bill sinks into his chair and scratches his chin. "Hmm. The gray aliens weren't in disguise, but the dragon was. I wonder what he's up to?"

Chapter 8
The Nine Underwater Cities

The sudden wealth of the Knights Templar is no mystery at all. In the middle of the 12th century, Pope Innocent II issued a papal bull, endorsing the Knights Templar and freeing them from any taxation. Taxes act like compound interest against the people, so the fewer taxes the better it is for the people. The Knights Templar decided to become bankers, compounding their money further. Albert Einstein said that compound interest is the most powerful force in the universe, and the biggest buildings in a city are usually banks. By making profit and not paying taxes, they became as rich as kings. One hundred fifty years after the Knights Templar began, King Philip IV pressured Pope Clement V to hunt them down. He didn't like the competition.

Harwell sits down with his new Osirian friends in the same conference room. General Hamilton, Asher and several others are there, as well. In the interest of popular support, the White House is still broadcasting the meetings all around the world.

Thinking of glistening underwater cities of light, Harwell offers L'lith a cup of coffee. "Tell us what Osiria looks like," he says.

She smiles. "Osiria would look a lot like Manhattan, if you turned it upside-down and each building were two hundred stories tall," L'lith explains. She brushes her chin with the back of her hand. "Of course, it's much larger than Manhattan . . . and not so spread-out. There are hundreds of buildings, all arranged in a thirty-mile-wide circle. One hundred million people live there."

Harwell nearly spits out his coffee. "One hundred **million**?!" he asks in astonishment. "Our entire country is that big!"

General Hamilton shoots a silencing look at Asher.

"Why haven't our submarines seen it, yet?" Harwell asks her. "Surely they saw all the lights."

The general shoots Asher another look.

L'lith laughs. "The lights are on the inside, not on the outside," she says. "The buildings look like a cross between a skyscraper and a bunker. The buildings are wide, angular and very deep. Since they are underground, you probably wouldn't notice them even if you used ground-penetrating sonar. They'd probably look like pieces of bedrock. All ten cities use the same idea: Many very tall buildings, buried deep in the ocean floor. There are nine other cities like Osiria, seven of which are for humans."

Harwell's freezes with his eyes open wide, like a deer caught in headlights. "There are aliens living on Earth?" he asks.

Asher keeps his mouth shut.

L'lith doesn't bat an eyelash. "Yes and no," she says. "The Lemurians live in two cities, and Foreign Nationals visit all the time."

Harwell makes no secret of his apprehension.

"You must keep in mind," she says, "that Lemurians evolved on Earth three hundred million years before humans even arrived. They'd 'met their neighbors' a long time ago."

Harwell slowly and timidly puts down his cup. "From **our** point of view, this is all very sudden," he says quietly, and clears his throat. "Tell me more about these cities. Where are they, and what are they called?"

She thinks for a moment and continues. "Pané Jia is east of New Zealand, Mu is west of Chile, Hesperides lies east of Paraguay, Eden is southeast of Africa and Kerguela lies west of Australia. Atlantis is just east of your state of Florida, Lemuria is just west of your state of California, Utsuro Buné is near Japan, Shambhala was abandoned and lies near India and Osiria is east of Cypress in the Mediterranean." She takes a sip of the coffee. "Mmm," she says. "I have something like this on my ship. It's very relaxing. Mu and Lemuria are Lemurian cities. Osiria was a blessing in disguise."

"Oh?" Harwell asks. "How is that?"

"At that time, Osiria was an island nation and a rival of Atlantis," she begins. "It . . . had an accident . . . and was destroyed. The people of Osiria were rescued at the same time as the Atlanteans. They eventually built an underwater city near the island and called it Atlantis, also. No human underwater cities would exist if it weren't for Osiria's harnessing of volcanic energy."

Several moments go by, until Harwell breaks the silence. "I'm sorry," he tells her, "but this alien thing is bothering me. I mean, we've found planets out there, but none of them have anything alive on them."

L'lith understands, and changes the subject. She looks around. "Don't tell G'brael I said this," she begins then loudly whispers, "but his people are exquisite engineers." Using her full voice again. "The spaceships of the past were shoddy and barely functional - virtual deathtraps that crashed all the time. They used spinning mercury, ion wind, magnets, gyroscopes, air pressure suspension and even rockets and airfoils. They consumed enormous amounts of power, too."

"These technologies had been in alien possession for millions of years," she continues, "but it's like they stumbled onto those things one day. Many of them still use those technologies, too. These aliens can mentally calculate exquisitely and remember in superb detail, but they are complete **idiots** about everything else. You have to see it to understand it. They've accumulated some wonderful technologies, but only because of the enormous amounts of

110

time that they have existed."

"G'brael's people changed all that," she tells him. "**True** anti-gravity, a sleek design, air and marine capability, simple operation and the use of minuscule amounts of power. It's like having the performance of a Ferrari with the simplicity of a video game. About 30 years ago, they came out with **genuine** mental controls. You don't even need to be a pilot, anymore. Just think it, and the ship will do it. Most races buy from them. Of course, somehow, some of these **idiot** aliens manage to crash one every now and then."

L'lith pretends to whisper a secret again. "Can you tell I don't like them?" she asks.

"Anyway," she says. "I think his people's success has made G'brael arrogant. He says that even government should be mathematically designed. He's living in a dream world! A good leader **takes** power! The public are like small children. They need to be **told** what to do. If they don't do it, then spank them and spank them hard. Certain people understand this better than others."

She takes another sip of her drink and changes the subject, yet again. "All intelligent species breathe oxygen," she tells him. "It takes breathable oxygen to make collagen and collagen glues multiple cells together. It reacts strongly while fairly stable and it . . ."

Asher breaks-in. "Why collagen?" he asks. "Why not something else? It **is** an alien planet, after all."

L'lith isn't offended by the interruption. "Some things, Mr. Asher," L'lith answers, "are universal. Collagen is one of them. So are having cells, using chlorophyll and a breathable oxygen atmosphere. Another universal thing is that breathable oxygen makes ozone. It's a simple reaction, but it always occurs in an atmosphere with breathable oxygen. We use that trait to find Earth-like planets."

She starts to sip her drink again, but decides to finish talking first. "I won't bore you with the details, but we simply look at the reflective spectrum of ozone . . . in the radio range, of course." She takes another sip of the coffee.

Asher can't sit still. He stands up and blurts out. "Ozone!" he cries. "That's brilliant!"

He turns to Harwell. "Mr. President," he says, "stars can't make ozone! There'd be no interference from them at all!"

Harwell leans back in his chair. "Don't we already do stuff like that?" he asks.

Asher is in his element. "Sort of, Sir, but not really. We map the sky with radio telescopes, we listen for signals and we sometimes look at the composition of stars but not like this. We have probably seen it and glossed right over it. We've focused on 'the wobble effect' and 'star dimming' when a planet gets in front of it, but none are Earth-like. They're all giant planets. None have breathable air, water or safe temperatures."

L'lith translates for Asher. "None have life," she tells Harwell.

Asher turns from L'lith back to Harwell. "Yes!" he agrees. "Yes! Ozone is made from breathable oxygen and only **plants** can make breathable oxygen! Receiving those radio frequencies is absolute and positive proof of alien life!"

L'lith puts her cup on the table. "I didn't realize you are so interested in alien life," she announces innocently. "Did G'brael tell you about the Reticulans?"

Harwell shrugs his shoulders while looking around.

Asher translates for L'lith this time. "The Grays, Mr. President." he says.

Harwell looks around then points to the door. "Oh!" he tells her. "They were just here."

"No, Mr. President," Asher says, breathing quietly to summon patience. "Those were the Lemurians." Asher turns to L'lith. "He never told us about the Reticulans."

"Well," she tells them, "they'll be your first problem. They won't like it if you leave this star system."

Harwell looks at her. "What do they care?" he asks.

L'lith picks up her cup and saucer, but does not raise them to her mouth. "The Lemurians and the Grays fought an enormous war more than 250 million years ago. The Lemurians tried using a new weapon using the heat from inside the Earth. The plan backfired, melting a huge area of the Earth's crust and causing a mass extinction. The Grays used the situation to their advantage by firing mass drivers. By the way, their mass drivers is why you have uranium deposits on the surface of Earth. I'm surprised that humans didn't notice that something **that** heavy didn't sink into the Earth a long time ago. It's like seeing a brick floating on water and **not** wondering why. The Lemurians escaped by building homes underwater."

Asher rubs his chin with his fingers. *I HAVE wondered about that,* he says to himself.

She lifts her cup to drink, again, but talks instead again. "The Grays banned any inhabitant of Earth from leaving this star system. Since that time, the Grays have developed robots that look **exactly** like themselves. Did G'brael tell you about S'lon?" She takes a quick sip of her drink.

Harwell looks to Asher "Yes," he answers for the

President. "A perfect android."

"Perfect?" she asks. "Yes and no. The biological Grays made too many of these androids. They were over-run and destroyed millions of years ago. Computers are notoriously literal. The biological Grays meant the Lemurians, but with the biological Grays gone there was no one to interpret an imperfectly written restriction for the android Grays."

Asher looks heart-broken. "Humans can't leave, either," he says. "Can we?"

"Just this star system," she confirms. "But Mars and Venus are fair game. Both are great terraforming projects! There was no need for us to do it, but we've thought about this for you to do . . . with our help, of course. Mars is an easier project, but it's still a really big project. Just put a lot of heavy material on over Mars. Asteroid iron will work nicely. We can just drop several of the bigger asteroids on the surface. That'll stretch the fabric of space and make the planet much heavier. Increased gravity will pull the atmosphere together and warm the air."

L'lith laughs to herself. "Of course, there's not much air to begin with," she comments. "Increased gravity will also increase pressure in the planet's core, warming it up and letting it generate a magnetic field. Then drop a few hundred water-ice asteroids on it, along with a few hundred nitrogen-ice asteroids. Let it sort itself out for a little while and you'll have a new planet!"

General P'al speaks for the first time. "It will need a large moon," he says with his ultra-deep voice.

L'lith turns her head to look at him, pauses for a few moments, then talks to the people in the room again. "Yes," she confirms. "The Lemurians tried to terraform Mars 23 million years ago. They got a lot of things right, but the things they got wrong messed up the whole project. They didn't increase the gravity then they tried to use two small moons to stabilize the planet. That method needs a lot less 'moon,' but it has to work precisely. It works great on paper, but not so well in practice. You can construct a large moon out of asteroid iron and Stannum, or simply drag another moon over to it. Triton is a good candidate. It'd be a good nitrogen source, too."

General Hamilton shakes his head. "What you're talking about sounds nice, but it's **preposterous**! We sometimes have trouble just getting into space; much less moving moons like they were marbles! If we were gods . . ."

L'lith cuts him off. "We **are** the gods," she says flatly.

The general stops dead in his tracks, and the room seems to echo with her words.

"And yes, we **can** move moons like they were marbles. All

of this is because of our technology . . . which we are giving to you. That makes **you** gods, too."

General Hamilton looks stunned, standing with his mouth partly open. He starts to say something then stops. He seems to think of something else, starts to say it and stops again. "Okay," he finally utters, and steps back a little.

A dull silence fills the room for about the millionth time today. Asher breaks it. "If we are gods now, then why are we stuck on Earth?"

"You have more immediate problems than the Grays, though," she warns.

Harwell must have dozed off through part of the conversation. "What?" he asks.

L'lith answers him. "When the Earth crosses the galactic plane," she explains. "Today. It will put pressure on Earth's planet core. Normally it's not a problem, but human activity has changed that. This time, pressure will relieve itself in a supervolcanic eruption . . . Yellowstone Park. With all of that happening at one time, the magnetic field will move. Sedona, Arizona, will be your new north pole . . . the **magnetic** north pole, that is. Water is weakly diamagnetic, and will follow the magnetic field. The Gulf of Mexico will split your country in two by flooding many of your states. Japan will be completely submerged and the Mediterranean Sea will nearly drain. That doesn't even include the acid rain or the ash cloud from the supervolcano."

Harwell decides to comment. "Maybe the ash cloud is a good thing," he says. "It can cool down our planet's Global Warming situation."

L'lith shoots a menacing look at him. "It'll **definitely** cool your planet down," she scolds him. "It'll block out most of the sunlight and it's warmth for nearly two years. There'll be acid rain, crops will fail, starvation will follow and people will freeze to death in the summer. But at least the planet will be cooler. All religions lie! Including the religion of Global Warming, or whatever you're calling it this week!"

"Climate Change," Asher tells her in a quiet voice.

"Weather!" she bellows. "That figures!"

Harwell tries to retract his comment. "I'm sorry. I . . ."

L'lith cuts him off, suddenly much calmer. "It wasn't you, Harwell," she apologizes. "It was me." She speaks with a stoic voice and her eyes glisten with tears, but none fall. "As much as I know and as much as I see, I can't do anything about it. This isn't **my** planet. It's yours. You aren't **my** people, you're G'brael's people. All I can do is protect the survivors."

She looks at Asher. "Do you see how your problems are more immediate than the Grays?"

He nods, and L'lith turns her attention back to Harwell. "We can take some of your people underwater with us," she says, "and we can relocate some of them underground on Mars. That'll keep them out of harm's way while it's being terraformed. But I'm afraid that we can't accommodate all of your people. Our underwater city is only designed for 100 million people, and we have people of our own. A lot of people will just have to stay here." She hangs her head. "Some of your people will survive this, but I'm sorry to say that some won't."

One of the aids thinks out loud. "It'll be like Hurricane Katrina all over again," he says.

L'lith agrees with him. "Unfortunately," she says, "it will be a **planetary** Hurricane Katrina. We have ships that can take all of you, but there's no **place** to take you. Until we dig underground homes for all of you, Mars is too dangerous. The Hephaes work fast; 24 hours a day and seven days a week, but it'll take them a decade to build eight **billion** underground homes. You don't have that long."

Harwell ventures a question. "What is that?" he asks.

"**Those**," she says, a fleeting flare of anger visible. She immediately lowers her voice, and takes a quick breath to calm herself. "Those are construction robots," she answers. "If we didn't have to build underground homes for you, we'd be able to save more of you. Maybe even all of you."

Harwell finally sees the answer. "Mr. Asher is right," he tells them. "What is the point in being gods if we're stuck here on Earth? If we could go to any planet in the galaxy, we could just go to a good one, wait for two years then come back."

L'lith smiles, as if waiting for **him** to ask that question. "We don't have much time so I'm going to tell you . . . in private . . . from leader to leader," she says.

"Everyone here can be trusted," he assures her.

She keeps her mouth closed, and points to the broadcast equipment. Lowering her head, she touches two fingers to her temple.

The room, the people, everything vanishes in an instant. Harwell finds himself walking with L'lith in the White House's Rose Garden. Snow covers the ground, the walkways are perfectly clear and the sun gleams in the wintery sky. He doesn't even realize there has been a transition. Everything seems perfectly natural. L'lith is still wearing her dress and armor while he wears a trench coat. Blowing lightly, the wind carries the smell of snowy air.

"Are you cold?" Harwell asks her.

She answers him without emotion. "I'm not concerned about the weather," she says. "The situation with the Grays is more serious than I mentioned earlier. Ears were listening at the time."

"I understand," he says.

L'lith clasps her hands together, nervously rolling them. "They're coming for you . . . all of you."

Harwell feels like his heart just fell into his stomach. He stops walking. "Wh . . . What do you mean?"

L'lith swallows. "G'brael put you in danger," she tells him, "but the danger was coming anyway. This way gives you a fighting chance."

Harwell tries to gulp, but his mouth is too dry. "Danger?" he hoarsely whispers.

She nods. "The Grays have two criteria for destroying a people," she tells him. "A means of destroying them, and a way of **getting** to them."

Harwell starts to say something, but she cuts him off.

"Intent doesn't matter to them," she tells him. "We're talking about robots. Remember?"

She obviously answered his question because he stays quiet and listens. "Your people became targets when your people created nuclear weapons."

Harwell starts to say something again, but she cuts him off again.

"They're robots!" she insistently tells him. "They don't **have** a pity gene!" He closes his mouth. "Now that you have a means of destroying them **and** a way of getting to them, your time is almost up. They will attack . . . now."

He rubs his clean-shaven face with one hand. "G'brael told me that this will be the greatest test that Mankind has ever faced," he says.

Agitated, L'lith tries to hide her feelings. She tightens her lips, and takes a deep breath. "He wasn't kidding," she feigns. "Was he?"

Harwell sighs deeply. "No, he wasn't," he replies, still cupping his face.

She noticeably sighs as well. "I tried to buy time by telling you how to terraform Mars," she says, "but I'm not sure it'll work in time."

Harwell sighs again. "How long do you think we have?" he asks.

L'lith looks at the pavement. "We're talking about machines," she says. "They don't sleep, there's no 'proper chain of command,' there's no paperwork to file and there's certainly no laziness." She sighs. "If they were biological I'd say two or three weeks, but with robots it'll be more like a two or three **days**. Maybe sooner."

Harwell sighs loudly, yet again. "I really need General Hamilton here to help me make military decisions," he tells her.

They start walking again. "Why?" she asks. "You're a perfectly capable man," she pushes. "You don't need such a violent . . . man . . . making military decisions for you."

While trying not to offend his new benefactor, Harwell defends his friend. "Alan Hamilton is not a violent man," he says. "He takes my ideas and turns them into something the troops can understand."

L'lith nods her head. "So you're saying," she says, "is that he simply regurgitates your orders then acts like he did you a favor."

Harwell looks at her, thinks for a few moments and then nods.

"I think he's a soulless creature that should be getting coffee for you," she tells him. "An evolved monkey like him doesn't deserve such a high-ranking position. Why don't you tell **me** your ideas? I know our starships and their abilities better than he would anyway."

Harwell hesitates for a split second, and then blurts out his thoughts to her. "I think we need to hit them first," he says. "Maybe if we hit them a little bit, they'll just leave us alone."

L'lith shakes her head. "No," she says. "You need to hit them so hard that they can't get up again - then kick them some more." She kicks her foot.

Harwell looks disturbed. "But those people!" he exclaims.

She musters patience with a quick breath. "They are **not** people," she reminds him. "They are robots. Machines . . . run amuck. And even if they **were** people, they're people that want to kill us . . . all of us. America isn't the only one in danger here, but only America has the skills to pull this off. That's why we came here. This isn't just a National Security issue; this is a **Planetary** Security issue. Americans and non-Americans alike will suffer the consequences if your people don't take action!"

Harwell looks at her face, but still seems disturbed by her plan, and she changes tactics. "We'll compromise," she says. "We can do something else. We'll destroy their ships so they can't get to us. We'll also destroy their factories so they can't build more ships." She smiles innocently.

Harwell smiles as well. "I like the second plan better," he tells her. "That would save hundreds or even thousands of lives."

L'lith doesn't say anything.

He thinks for a minute. "Okay," he says. "Let's do it!"

L'lith smiles. "I think that will be a very popular idea," she tells him. She immediately gets down to business. "How many nuclear missiles do you have?" she asks.

He begins to answer. "Actually," he starts, and then realizes what she asked. "Wait a second! What?!"

She explains. "If you detonate a nuclear missile high in the atmosphere," she tells him, "it creates an EMP, Electro-Magnetic Pulse. Any circuitry that isn't shielded well enough will become useless. Spaceships, weapons and communications will all become paperweights. That'll tremendously reduce casualties. We'll use a lot of missiles and take out their entire operation."

L'lith talks to herself. "It doesn't matter how many you have," she says. "We'll just ride in on our huge spaceships and simply take them from other countries. This **is** Planetary Security, after all. They all have to contribute."

Deeply conflicted, Harwell wrestles with the idea. "We should ask, first" he tells her. "Give them a chance to **volunteer** the missiles."

L'lith sneers at the idea. "You can always count on people to do the wrong thing," she rebuts. "Take them and be done with it!"

Harwell seems to struggle with the idea for a few moments before accepting it. "We'll put your people in Osirian ships to launch a massive pre-emptive strike," she tells him. "To make the strike big enough, we'll use every nuclear weapon on this planet."

She takes his tentative agreement, and expands the plan back to her original thought. "In case their equipment is shielded," she says, "we'll just land a few of those punches. That will rid you and the rest of the galaxy, of the oppressive Gray Empire once and for all."

There is definite glee in her voice. "That'll have the added effect," she continues, "of leveling the playing field here on Earth. **No one** on this planet will have nuclear weapons."

Any conflict Harwell felt is gone now. "I feel better already," he says.

L'lith stops and turns to face him. "You shouldn't let other people tell you what to do." she tells him.

His face drops. "I know," he says. "People make fun of me, and think I don't understand."

The soft side of her shows itself once again. "But they're wrong," she tells him. "Aren't they? You're smarter than people give you credit."

Harwell nods. "My old boss underestimated me," he tells her. His blue eyes meet her green ones. "I certainly showed him. I'm the President now!"

She starts walking again. "And making military decisions **completely** on your own," she says. "It feels good. Powerful. Doesn't it?"

He walks with her. "Yes, it does," he says. "I feel like a kid who took his mother's car and got away with it."

L'lith looks at him. "America has already achieved global dominance," she tells him, "and now it has the opportunity for **galactic** dominance. It just needs a strong and forceful leader to make it happen. Can you be forceful?"

Harwell puffs out his chest a bit. "They won't know what hit them," he answers. "Any of them."

L'lith smiles. *'Compromise,'* she thinks, *means that he agrees with ME. She touches two fingers to her temple again.*

Later That Night

Alone in his office, Dr. Livingston marks on a world map

that lay on the table behind his computer chair. A picture of L'lith and General P'al lay next to accounts of drawings of dragons, and ancient eyewitness accounts of them. He continues to replay the digital broadcast of L'lith's comments about the underwater cities.

Years ago he realized that saying his thoughts out loud helps him to get new ideas. "Most of the underwater cities lay on the Northern and the Southern 30° latitudes," he says to himself. "I wonder why."

The computer's voice alerts him. "Your data has finished compiling," it announces.

Underwater Cities

He whirls his chair around. "Oh! Good!" he says. "I remember having seen tiny ozone signatures on these reports when I was an undergraduate, but didn't think anything of it at the time."

He mutters as he opens a colorful, 3-D graph of radio frequencies. There's a lot of them. "I must be an idiot. I could have gotten a Nobel Prize! It didn't occur to me that this was proof of alien life. Well . . . plant life, at least. Oxygen-1 is all over the place, but only plants can turn it into oxygen-2 . . . breathable oxygen. There's more than one way to make it, so I'll look at a consequence of breathable oxygen to avoid false positives. That's an ozone layer in the sky."

Dr. Livingston frowns. "I can see that the radio frequencies for ozone are here, and I can tell the computer which ones to select, but it's all lumped together. I can't tell from which areas of the sky that these radio frequencies are coming."

Thoughtful for a moment, he suddenly sits up in his chair, opens a new computer window and starts feverishly typing. "This will be fun," he says. "Make the ozone radio frequencies to display in a sky blue color, then route the data to the university's planetarium."

He types a bit more, finishing the transfer. He stands up, stretches and looks at the clock. "Whoa!" he says. "It's midnight! No wonder I feel so stiff! Well, I guess no one will object to my little game, then!"

Lazily gathering a few things, he walks out of the office door.

As expected, the planetarium is completely deserted. It is a medium-sized, round room with several rows of auditorium-style folding seats arranged in a big circle. Almost everything is black, except the white, half-dome-shaped ceiling above him. It's like being inside a globe. Dr. Livingston types a few commands on the planetarium computer's keyboard and the room lights suddenly dim, showing a remarkably realistic representation of twilight.

Stars begin to appear on the sunken, round ceiling as the scene progresses into night. "Okay," he says as he leans over and types on the keyboard again. He looks up, looks back at the computer screen, then looks up again while squinting. "The data I sent is displaying up there, but I can't see any difference. Let me try this."

He types a few more commands and the stars fade away, leaving dozens upon dozens of minuscule points of blue on the ceiling.

"Oh my God!" he gasps. "It was here the whole time and I never saw it! This is proof . . . solid proof of alien life." He stands there, daydreaming about the Nobel Prize he could have won, then snaps back to reality. "Alien plant life, that is."

Livingston stares at the blue dots on the ceiling for a few

minutes. "Naturally-occurring oxygen isn't breathable, but plants use photosynthesis to convert carbon dioxide into sugars while converting water into breathable oxygen. So where there is ozone, there is breathable oxygen. Where there is breathable oxygen, there are alien plants. Where there are alien plants, there **might** be alien animals . . . or something even higher."

He unconsciously walks to one of the theater chairs. Just as he starts to sit down, he jumps up again; darting to the computer. "This is the sky in Earth's Northern Hemisphere," Livingston mutters.

After setting the Viewing Location to Sydney, Australia, the blue dots on the ceiling move, almost as though someone is spinning a giant globe.

"But we're talking about a planet in the Reticulum constellation, and that's in Earth's Southern Hemisphere."

Dr. Livingston turns on the Constellation Identifier to help him, and quickly finds the correct constellation, nearly in the center of the sky. There is a blue dot outside the Reticulum constellation itself, near the Horologium constellation.

"Hmm," he mumbles. He types on the computer's keyboard again and the blue dot quickly enlarges to be a couple of feet across, with a white star right next to it. "Zeta-2 Reticuli," he announces under his breath. He cocks his head back. "I've heard of that star."

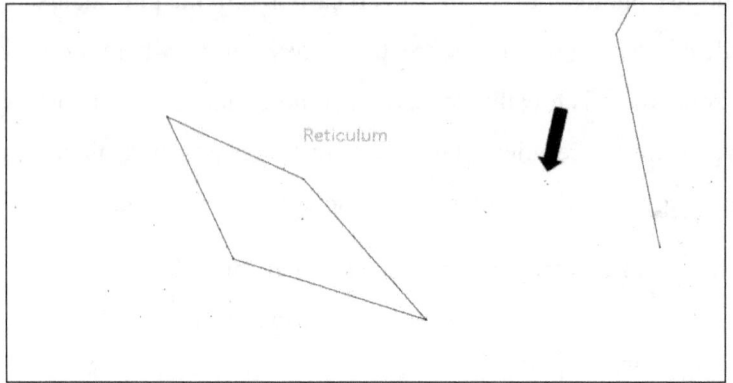

Zeta-2 Reticuli

Chapter 9
Preparing For War

A country that splits into two countries will scuffle with the other side and then escalate into a war. Eventually the 'more aggressive' side will overtake the other. It's a cycle. Oaths of allegiance, personal ridicule, second-class citizenship and financial turmoil will go on and on for generations. Secession is just not worth the price. But a country that splits into three, five or seven new countries (an odd number) can prevent such an agonizing cycle.

Harwell conducts a debriefing without General Hamilton. "Ansibles will give us real-time reconnaissance from modified comets," Harwell tells a small group of high-ranking military officers.

He stands near a large screen, pointing at it and explaining his plan.

"A team will go to the Gray's star system and install dozens of sensors and receivers into natural comets, while they is still near the outer planets. They will record everything. Normally that would help us plan the attack, but this is not a normal situation."

A colonel is the lowest-ranking officer in the room. "With respect, Mr. President," he says. "You're talking about updates and not reconnaissance. It would take months or years for this type of information to help us."

A two-star general speaks. "Mr. President," he says, "why

isn't this a normal situation? Overwhelming success comes from good intelligence and a lot of planning."

Harwell ignores the Colonel, briefly looking at the CIA Director who had been lurking in the corner. "Already done," he says, only answering the Two Star. "These are sensors of Osirian design. It won't take months."

The Colonel nervously swallows before offering advice. "Mr. President," he hesitantly offers, "sensors can be placed on natural comets as you said. They can then help identify military targets and avoid civilians. A single nuclear weapon exploded several miles above each target will cripple their defenses with EMPs . . ."

Harwell cuts him off. "I've heard that plan, Colonel." he says. "It's too slow, and I think it's for wimps." Harwell raises his voice. "This is the **Big One**, People! The survival of the human race, and every other race out there, is in our hands . . . right now! Others have tried half-assed attacks like that! They're dead now! <u>All</u> of them!"

He stops for a moment, then speaks in a normal voice. "The enemy is deceptive and cunning," he tells them. "Military-looking targets are actually decoys while civilian-looking houses launch starfighters. These are robots, not flesh and blood creatures. There are no civilians and there are no true casualties. Nothing can be off-limits. Surprise. . . Surprise will be our greatest weapon. The modified comets will help us to identify targets. Military bases with obvious fighter craft must be destroyed. We don't want them able to hit back. I want to hit them with a sledgehammer! Then hit them again and again!"

General Hamilton hurriedly walks into the room. "I apologize, Mr. President," he pants. "I wasn't informed about this meeting."

Harwell walks over to him and shakes his hand. "That's quite alright, General," he says, smiling. "You weren't invited."

The general starts to laugh but sees the look in Harwell's eyes. He breaks away. "Y . . . You're serious. Aren't you?" he says.

"Aren't you, **Sir**," Harwell corrects him.

The general steps back a little. "Yes, Sir," he says, choosing his words carefully. "I'm sorry, Mr. President. It won't happen again, Sir."

Harwell is still smiling. "You're dismissed, General," he says.

As Harwell starts to turn to leave, General Hamilton

speaks up. "Mr. President," he says, "you are planning a preemptive nuclear attack on millions of people."

Harwell turns to face the general and closes his eyes. "Robots," he says and then opens his eyes again. "Robots, General. I'm planning to turn millions of machines off. Does that warrant your presence? This mission, and this mission alone, is what it will take to keep these machines from ravaging our country or our planet. Again . . . you are dismissed."

Harwell turns and walks away.

General Hamilton stands there for a few moments with his mouth partly open.

He hears Harwell telling the others. "We're going to launch every nuke the Human Race has ever built. I want that place to be a molten ball of . . . planet by the time we're done with it!"

General Hamilton notices the CIA Director, pauses and finally turns to leave the room.

At Asher's Apartment

Asher goes home: excited, fearful and exhausted. He immediately logs in to a chat room and finds his friends, Joe and Tex.

```
Asher:  President Harwell isn't one of us anymore.
```

Both answer at the same time. Tex is being his usual smart-ass self while Joe is being naïve.

```
Tex:    I didn't know you two were buddies.

Joe:    How so?
```

Asher ignores Tex' comment.

```
Asher:  He's bought all of that stuff: hook, line
        and sinker.

Asher:  I think something else is going on.
```

Tex tries to be serious, for once.

```
Tex:    Why do you think that?
```

Asher types feverishly.

```
Asher:  It just doesn't feel right. L'lith is hiding
        something.

Tex:    From what you've said, they showed up on a
        special day, told us about the past and
        predicted a future that's PROBABLY right.

Tex:    You're worried because. . . what?
```

Asher realizes that he sounds like he's just minutes away from wearing a tin foil hat, like those nut-jobs on TV.

```
Asher:  It may be a paranoid speculation on my part,
        but the most convincing place to put a lie
```

```
         is directly between two truths.
```

They reply at the same time.

```
Joe:    I see.

Tex:    Oh? Like what?
```

Asher explains.

```
Asher:  G'brael is like a mentor or a professor.

Asher:  He pulls answers out of you, while L'lith
        just gives you the answers and tells you to
        pick a fight.
```

The two reply at the same time, again.

```
Tex:    That isn't good.

Joe:    I see your point.
```

Asher pauses then asks.

```
Asher:  Can you two meet me, so we can talk?
```

Tex seems to jump.

```
Tex:    You mean In Real Life??

Joe:    I'm not sure that's such a good idea.
```

He's suspicious.

```
Asher:  What's the big deal, you guys?

Asher:  We've been chatting for two years.

Asher:  I doubt there are ANY secrets left.

Tex writes, but Joe doesn't reply.
```

```
Tex:    Why don't you just talk to us here?
```

Asher pushes a bit more.

```
Asher:  It's just not the same.
```

```
Asher:  This has been an enormous day for us all. I
        REALLY don't want to be left alone with my
        thoughts.
```

```
Tex:    You won't.
```

```
Tex:    We'll go on and on and on and... until you
        fall asleep on the keyboard.
```

Asher doesn't mince words.

```
Asher:  I feel overwhelmed and I need you guys to
        level me out.
```

```
Asher:  I need to see your faces.
```

There's a pause and Joe finally writes:

```
Joe:    Okay, Asher. Just remember that you are our
        best friend in the world.
```

```
Asher:  Now you're scaring me.
```

Tex tries to lessen Asher's anxiety, but can't resist a
chance to be a smart-ass.

```
Tex:    It's not that bad. We'll meet at the coffee
        shop on G Street NW and 22nd.
```

```
Tex:    I'll be wearing a coat.
```

```
Asher:  Very funny, Tex. It's December.
```

Asher: Everyone's wearing a coat.

Tex: Okay. Okay. A green coat.

Joe: We'll all look for the green coat.

Chapter 10
The Meeting

(The Same Evening)

As much as feminists wish it was true, women have never been pawns. They have shaped Human Civilization from the beginning, but fewer and fewer are aware of that strength. Voting's strength is minuscule compared with motherhood's strength. Ask any new bride about her mother-in-law's influence. Motherhood decreases as political involvement increases . . . and Mankind suffers from its absence. A mother shapes her child into exactly what SHE wants and rarely what the father wants. Presidents, kings and emperors all have mothers. The hand that rocks the cradle is the hand that rules the world

As Asher walks into the coffee shop, he sees that there aren't many people inside. He looks around for his two friends, but only sees an older man with a black jacket, two young women sitting together and a shorthaired blond woman ordering at the counter. *Not here yet,* he thinks as he walks past her and finds a place to sit down.

He notes that the blond woman is ordering hot chocolate. *She'll need it,* he thinks. *It's 15 degrees out there!*

After waiting for a few minutes, he notices that one of the two young women is staring at him. *Was this a girl I knew back in college?* he wonders.

Realizing she's been caught. "Asher?" she asks with a slight drawl.

He tries to be polite. "I'm sorry," he says. "Do I know you?"

"It's me," she tells him. "Tex."

Asher **cannot** be more shocked. "No," he says. "This is a joke. Right? The guys are messing with me."

The other girl turns around and he recognizes her immediately.

"Joanne? What are you doing . . ." he starts to ask her. He pauses for a second then understands. "Joe," he says, almost like an accusation.

Joanne nearly jumps out of her chair to embrace him. He holds his hands out, like he's keeping her at bay, and she stops. "Two years online?" he starts. "And two years ago. Yes, our date was two years ago. **Now** I find out that you've been stalking me ever since then."

Joanne keeps her distance. "I'm so, so sorry, Asher," she tells him, nearly in tears. Other people take notice of the scene. "What can I do to make it up to you?" she begs.

"Just have sex with him," Tex comments. "Everything will be forgiven by morning."

He glares at her.

"What?!" Joanne demands.

"It's what guys want, anyway," Tex sneers, but then realizes something and gasps. "Or is this why you liked him in the first place? Real men have feelings, but rarely show them. These north-easterners have them **and** show them . . . but this one's different."

Only then does Asher notice that Tex is wearing a green coat.

"Listen," she tells him. "Joanne has dated lots of guys, and most of them are lying horn-dogs. She said she liked you because you were completely honest, but you weren't living up to your potential. We went incognito to help you, but it went farther than we intended and we're sorry. That's the honest truth."

Asher was about to remind her of the 'honest truth' coming from a liar, but knows it won't change anything. He sighs, and hangs his head in defeat. "I've told things to both of you that are . . . beyond embarrassing. There's a lot more to this than just a gender thing. I am truly, truly embarrassed and truly, truly hurt. I believed in you and trusted you. And you deceived me. Both of you."

"We're sorry," Tex says.

"But believe it or not," Joanne adds, "we both think you're really, really sweet."

"Thanks," he absently mutters and then turns around and walks to the door.

Joanne tries to stop him. "What did you want to talk about?" she asks.

Asher stops and turns around. "Well," he tells her, "it could be about L'lith's conspiracy for interplanetary war or my ex-girlfriend stalking me or my best friends deceiving me about more than one thing. Take your pick." He turns around again to walk out.

Tex tries to lighten the mood. "Is that the Little Green Men Conspiracy, the Humans in UFOs Conspiracy or the Little Gray Robots Conspiracy?"

Annoyed, Asher turns around. "Not funny," he tells her.

Joanne seizes her chance. "How can we help?" she asks. "What can we do?"

"Besides sex," Tex injects.

They both glare at her this time.

She holds her hands up. "Sorry. Sorry. It just comes out sometimes."

That's definitely the Tex I know, Asher thinks. "I'm really tired," he tells them. "It's going to be insanely busy at work tomorrow and I need to rest. I'll decide what to do, and talk to you guys in a few days." Before anyone can stop him, he quickly turns around and walks out of the shop.

Tex turns to Joanne. "He'll get over it," she says. "And if he doesn't, you can still offer sex to him."

It starts snowing as Asher slowly walks home. *It's more of the same,* he thinks.

The snow makes crunching sounds under his feet. Normally he likes the sounds, but right now he doesn't even want to listen.

I'm honest with other people, and they deceive me, he thinks.

He walks across the street walkways without looking for cars. *Maybe I'll get lucky and get hit,* he thinks.

The streets are vacant, covered in a fine layer of fresh snow and there isn't a single tire track in sight.

He suddenly stops walking, right in the middle of the street. *Wait! I sound like such a self-pitying dweeb!*

Asher looks around. *There may be losers in bars, but not everyone who goes to a bar is a loser.*

He starts walking in a new direction. *Tex was right, even*

though he . . . she . . . didn't mean to be right. Drown my sorrows in a few drinks, then pick up a chick. Hell! At this point, I'd pay for one! I'm a government worker! I've got money!

Inside the Bar

It looks just like Asher has imagined it: lowered lights, country music, people laughing and a pool table in the corner. Asher gets a beer at the bar, and sits close to the pool table. He nurses his beer, and quietly watches the game: studying the rules, the geometry of the game and the methods for making really good plays.

After a few more beers, two hours of watching the game and playing the game in his head; Asher feels confident enough to try it himself. Winning one game would give his confidence a boost, but winning numerous games would give his status in the bar a boost! He would become a **magnet** for women!

He notices a young woman, probably barely old enough to come inside of a bar, sporadically coming to the pool table, beating one of the rough-looking men, then blending back into the crowd. Asher knows what she is . . . a pool shark.

Logic tells him to stay away from the young woman, but

his hormones tell him otherwise. She has shiny, medium-length brown hair, blue eyes and a gorgeous body . . . and her Daisy Duke shorts show off her smooth and slender legs. He watches her beat another unsuspecting man, then swiftly moves in to talk to the young woman, only half a head shorter than himself. "Most of these people aren't old," he tells her, "but it's nice to see someone about my age."

She looks startled. "Oh!" she gasps. "Yeah! Good to see you, too!"

The young pool shark starts to walk away. "Do you want to play?!" he quickly asks.

She turns around, and fakes a smile. "You're new to the bar scene. Aren't ya?" she asks, as her blue eyes size him up.

Asher looks down at his clothes: a knit shirt, fresh blue jeans and tennis shoes. He looks back up at her. "How can you tell?" he playfully asks.

The young woman smiles. "You're nice . . . and funny," she tells him. "I like that." She brushes a lock of hair behind her ear. "I don't want to take your money," she says, before turning to walk away again.

Asher can tell from her body language that she does **want** to take his money, and is playing a different kind of game with him. He turns it around, though. "Then we won't play for money," he tells her. "If I win, you tell me your name."

She turns around. "That's easy," she tells him. "It's Mary. See? You already won!" She turns to leave, yet again.

"No," Asher refuses. "Your real name."

The young pool shark turns around again, this time without the smile, and walks up to him. "What is your name?" she asks.

He tosses it back into her court. "Play me, and find out . . . maybe."

Her face loses all sense of humor. Picking up a pool-stick, she chalks the tip. "Three minutes," she tells him. "I'll know your name in three minutes."

Still being coy. "Maybe," he answers, as he walks around the table. "Maybe not."

A humorless 'Mary' racks up the balls, then feigns generosity. "I'll even let you go first," she tells him.

Asher chalks the tip of his pool-stick. "Thanks," he tells her. He chalks his left hand, then places the cue ball directly on the pool table's mark. Conscious of his body's position, he leans over the pool table, and takes aim. He smacks the cue ball dead in its center, sending it directly at the collection of balls. It hits the middle of the yellow-striped 1 ball, sending the other balls . . . about two inches.

'Mary' starts to laugh, then quickly covers it up with a fake cough.

Asher's embarrassed. "These balls have more mass than I realized," he tells her.

She nods. "Yes," she manages amidst her coughing. "More mass."

Her coughing spurt goes away. "Normally," 'Mary' tells him, "that's a breaking foul." She takes her turn, anyway, striking the cue ball hard, and sending the balls all over the tabletop. A solid green-colored ball falls into a corner pocket. "Solids," she announces. 'Mary' gleefully slinks around the pool table, aims her pool-stick and sinks a solid red-colored ball. "We can stop all this, if you tell me one thing," she tells him.

Asher plays more mind games with her. He shakes his head, pretending to talk to himself. "Three moves into the game," he says, "and she wants to quit so she can learn more about me."

Visibly annoyed, she aims for a solid blue-colored ball, shoots, and the cue ball bounces off the two rails of the corner pocket; **barely** missing the shot. 'Mary' is briefly upset by the mistake, but only briefly. "Your turn," she says.

Asher chalks the tip of his pool-stick again, and chalks his hand again. Leaning over the table, he lines the cue ball up with the 10 ball. Striking it with a lot more force than last time, the 10 ball skates into the corner pocket.

"Nicely done," she announces. "An easy shot, but you did well."

Asher's not sure if that was a compliment, or an insult.

'Mary' points to the 15 ball. "How about that one?" she baits.

He shakes his head. "No," he says, sticking to his plan. "There are too many balls around it." He lines the cue ball up with the 12 ball, and hits it lightly. The slow-moving cue ball grazes the 12 ball on its left side and drops it in the side pocket. "I've been carefully watching you and other pool players for hours," he says, pointing his hand toward her.

"This," he says, holding his hand over the table, "This is geometry. I'm good at geometry. This is also physics. I'm good at physics, too. But this is also about half a dozen other subjects that I don't know very well. That's where observation, and experience come in."

'Mary' gapes at him, aghast at his nerdiness. "Are you serious?? Just play!"

Asher has heard that before, and doesn't say another word. He turns around, lines up another ball, shoots and sinks the 9 ball. Not hesitating, he walks around the table, lines up again, shoots and sinks the 13 ball. He smiles as he stands up.

She leans up against a wooden post. "You're pretty lucky," she tells him.

His smile brightens. "Lucky? Maybe," Asher walks around the table, talking like a college professor. "In my . . . boring . . . observations, I noticed small inconsistencies from perfect geometry. The tiny imperfections in the rails or in the felt, make this table unique," he says, holding his hand over the table again. "Knowing where those imperfections are located gives me an edge over other players. It's not much, but it's an edge."

Asher is facing away from the door, but 'Mary' can see two women walking inside. She smiles like the cat that ate the canary. "I'm gonna put this bet into high gear," she starts. "If you sink the 8 ball on this very next shot, I'll go home with you."

He grins from ear to ear.

"If not," 'Mary' tells him, "then you have to leave the bar. Of course, you could always leave with one of those two, instead."

She points to the two women, who are already getting a lot of attention. "Recognize what they are?" she asks.

He stares at the women, then turns back to 'Mary.' "Prostitutes?" he asks in a lowered voice.

She looks at the women. "Oh yes," she answers. "There are more hookers in D.C. than Vegas and A.C., combined. They're a lot more discrete here, though."

Asher leans over the table, then looks back at 'Mary.' "No pressure," she tells him. He looks over at the two women, carefully lines up the cue ball and shoots.

Back at His Apartment

Asher wakes up the next morning . . . alone. "I'm glad I drank all that water when I got home last night," he says to himself. "Otherwise those four beers might have really gotten to me!" Not having a roommate gives him an immense amount of freedom, but that also means that he has no one to talk to about his problems.

Talking to himself helps. "I might have won, but I also saw Mary's face. She didn't **want** me. She just wanted to distract me. At least I found out her real name . . . Emily."

Suddenly exasperated, he sighs. "Now a bigger problem.

'The guys' are actually 'the girls,'" he says to himself as he stumbles out of bed. "What is **with** all these women lying to men?! Or are they just lying to guys like me?"

He sighs again. The computer grabs his attention as he walks to the kitchen. He normally chats online during breakfast, but not today. Chatting with unidentified people has been a snake in the grass, and has already bitten him once.

He glares at the inanimate machine. "It won't happen twice," he says. "I won't do it."

Asher walks to the bathroom, turns the water on and talks to his reflection in the mirror, trying to accept the new situation. "They haven't changed. They're just like guys, but they're actually girls." He half-heartedly smiles at the mirror.

He suddenly bursts out, yelling at his reflection. "Oh! Who am I kidding?! They lied to **me**! They hurt **me**! After two years, I didn't **know**?! The clues were right in front of me! I couldn't even pick up a hooker last night! What kind of a guy am I?!"

Asher takes a deep breath and closes his eyes. His head sinks, and he calmly releases the breath. "A nice guy," he answers himself. He raises his head again as the foggy glass begins to mask his reflection.

He wipes the mirror and sighs again. "I can't help who I

am," he says. "It's a curse when you're a young man and a blessing when you're an older man. I'll forgive them, but not too quickly. It'll take time to regain my trust. Yeah. That sounds good. I'll tell them that."

Chapter 11
Spaceship School

Antarctica is unique and mysterious. The entire continent is constantly frozen so it can't generate clouds hefty enough to snow or even to rain. The Earth's axis tilts it away from the sun, and it's nighttime for six months out of the year. With practically no thunderstorms or precipitation, the entire continent is a frozen desert. Since lightning and sunlight help convert breathable oxygen into ozone, there SHOULD be no mystery as to why Earth's ozone layer thins over this continent.

Four pilots arrive in a hangar at Whiteman Air Force Base in Missouri. A folding table sits in front of rows of folding chairs arranged neatly. The table has a blue cloth and coves several objects. Other folding tables sit behind the chairs, laden with coffee and doughnuts.

The pilots gather close to the food. They have not been told anything at all and have helped themselves to doughnuts as more pilots arrive. Soon there are dozens of pilots there, drinking coffee and talking.

A man, dressed in black Osirian battle armor, walks toward the front. The pilots rush to take their seats. The Osirian is not as tall as General P'al - normal-sized, with brown hair and brown eyes.

He waits for all the men to sit down. "Gentlemen," he tells them, "my name is K'ler, and I am going to instruct you in anti-gravity flight and Faster-Than-Light physics. The first thing is that this is how **our** ships work. Not every race does things the same way and sometimes not at all the same way."

K'ler

He speaks without much of an accent, but with abrupt words, like someone who once spoke German.

One man immediately raises his hand. "Sir," he asks, "why are you training **us** to fly **your** ships."

The instructor straightens himself. "That is a good question, Major . . . Donnelly," he says. "One with a complicated answer. This is a preemptive, surprise attack. The rest of the galaxy needs to know that it was **you** who did it and not us."

"But why?" he asks with an almost child-like curiosity. "Why would anyone believe that humans developed anti-gravity and Faster-Than-Light spaceships practically overnight?"

K'ler smirks. "Humans do amazing things all the time," he counters. The hangar murmurs with disbelief. "Anti-gravity is so simple that a man can create it in his garage, much like the first airplane. As was the automobile before that and the telegraph before that . . . so on and so forth. Right now there is probably some man, somewhere, that is upset because he figured it all out and we just swooped in one day and beat him to it! That happens more often than you realize."

Major Donnelly looks around at the other pilots, but they are all as clueless as him. "I understand what you're saying about invention," he says, "but what do you mean about the rest of the galaxy and us?"

"The entire galaxy," he begins, "has known about Humanity for a long time. Lemurians, Reticulans and others all evolved from one of the first animal groups on their planet, the Arthropods. Since evolution **ends** when sentience begins, they never evolved beyond short, gray creatures with blue blood. With most aliens having such a similar form, and such an **ancient** form, you probably think of those aliens as looking alike."

Another man raises his hand and stands up, fidgeting nervously. "Sir," he starts. "First of all, what does 'sentience' mean? And second, do you mean they literally have blue blood?" He sits down as fast as he can.

K'ler looks at the floor, then raises his head before answering. "Sentience means 'consciousness' or 'self-awareness,'" he tells the young man. "And yes, their blood is literally blue. It is based on copper."

"Shouldn't it be green?" he asks from his chair.

K'ler laughs quietly. "You watch too much television," he tells him, then speaks to the whole group. "Their blood is based on copper two, not copper one. They breathe oxygen, just like you do, and breathable oxygen is two. There are **many** species of short, gray aliens. They have been around for millions and millions of years. Sentience usually happens only once on a planet, sometimes twice. It is rare, but it happens. One time it happened three times on one planet. The people of the galaxy were absolutely amazed . . . until Earth. Past and present, it has happened here more than twenty times: All the whale species but none of the sharks, all the dolphin species but none of the fish, all of the elephant species but no other pachyderms, all the great ape species but none of the monkeys. Even a few of the bird species are sentient. That puts things in perspective, does it not?"

"God in Heaven has touched this planet," he tells them, "and everyone in the galaxy knows that. God's artistry, compared to Leonardo Da Vinci's, is like comparing a Rembrandt painting to a stick figure drawing. There is no comparison. Humans are God's divine gifts to the **entire** galaxy. Some alien races try to hybridize with humans, making the offspring look like humans. There may be more or less holy places on Earth for humans, but to the rest of the galaxy **Earth** is a holy place."

No one in the group says another word.

K'ler continues. "Many alien races make pilgrimages to see it. No one in the galaxy is surprised by **anything** that humans do." He starts to change subjects but decides against it. "You do not realize how close you are to matching alien technology," he tells them. "All it takes is one successful man in his garage for you to begin to believe."

K'ler waits a minute, letting the silence dominate the mood of the hangar floor before beginning his lecture.

"Okay!" he suddenly announces. "Back to the original subject!"

The pilots get their pens and paper ready.

"There are two major types of spaceships," he tells them, "those that can travel to other stars and those that cannot. You might think it is odd that some spaceships cannot travel to other stars, but think of boats or airplanes. You would not sail a rowboat to China or fly a Cessna to Africa, so why would you fly any old spaceship to Proxima Centauri?"

"Shape is the key," he continues. "Spaceships with Faster-Than-Light ability, FTL, have at least one side that is domed or shaped like a pie plate. It is more correct to think of it as a satellite dish. An FTL spaceship does not just have one big anti-gravity generator; it has many small ones. They work similar to hydrogen balloons, although each generator can magnify the other ones. Also, anti-gravity generators are far more powerful than hydrogen balloons, even though the generators are nothing more than a rod and a tube, a piston and a cylinder. We use a substance called Stannum to line these generators, these piston and cylinder devices, to produce both gravity **and** anti-gravity. If the piston travels in one direction then it is generating gravity, but if it travels the opposite direction then it is generating **anti**-gravity. These generators are very simple, but they are so powerful that a soda can-sized generator can easily lift an automobile. Also, most of them **look** like soda cans."

He removes the blue cloth and reaches for a pentagon-shaped, three-foot-wide piece of metal laying on the table. "We also cover our spaceships with panels like this one, which are made of Stannum." He holds up the silvery panel. A few concentric pentagons adorn it. "Stannum is an alloy, a blend of metals, not just one. Also, there are bubbles of various gases inside the alloy, similar to your Styrofoam. Is quite light. The air bubbles expand when we apply electricity."

He connects two wires to it. The panel suddenly glows with a soft-blue color.

The men gasp.

K'ler sighs noticeably, pauses for a moment, then continues. "I am using such a crude means of applying electricity to demonstrate this. Applying electricity with 5th dimensional channels is much more efficient and far more effective. Various metals are blended with the Stannum to make them glow different colors. This one has selenium, but

5th dimensional channels can ignite one metal while ignoring the metal right next to it. In other words, we can change the spaceship's color whenever we want."

He continues. "Other spaceships have strontium, iron, sodium, boron, potassium or none at all," he says. "One that has no embedded metals glows with a white color. The more power we give to it, the brighter it glows. It can look very bright at night. These panels are not necessary for flight, but they make the spaceship unique. It is similar to applying paint to an airplane."

"Electrified Stannum," he says, "acts like a force field against water."

He demonstrates by squirting the metal panel with water from a spray bottle. It sprays at the panel, but seems to hit an invisible barrier several inches from the panel, then simply falls to the ground.

"We can travel to **any** ocean depth without concern. When in the air, these panels are not as necessary but are still activated randomly because of water in the air. Humidity can slow a aircraft more than you might realize. We randomize their activation by fading their light, brightening it, fading it again, and so forth. It is similar to dimming and brightening a lightbulb in your house, but there are hundreds of millions of them. An activated panel next to a non-activated one looks black, just like a bright object next to a dimmer object. Sun Spots are a good example."

K'ler stops for a moment, like he just remembered something mundane. "I assume you understand that concept."

The pilots clamor something of an answer.

"Good," he says, not really caring if it's true or not. "People tell us that when they see these panels on our ships, it lookslike the scales of a flying reptile. That is probably where all these 'dragon' and 'flying serpent' myths come from."

"Although these panels are made of the same material," he continues, "they have nothing to do with anti-gravity. A satellite dish-shaped roof makes the ship extraordinarily stable. Imagine spreading hundreds of hydrogen balloons in the shape of a satellite dish, above a rowboat. Now imagine evenly attaching each of them to that rowboat. Now you understand."

"A person will never see a spaceship bank, or lean into a turn," he says. "It does not have to do so, since it is floating on the gravity field of the planet, which is level. The Stannum walls of the spaceship protect the occupants from the inertial force, or any force it endures, just like an airplane's cockpit protects a pilot from the forces that his airplane endures. The spaceship can accelerate to **<u>any</u>** speed it wants, as quickly as it wants. **<u>There</u> <u>are</u> <u>no</u> <u>consequences</u>**.”

“When the spaceship gets into space it will turn on its side,” he says, motioning with his hands. The small silver disk sitting on the folding table springs to life, and a hologram of a UFO emerges. The pilots gasp, and K’ler stops for a moment.

“Your people experience wonderment with **<u>every</u>** technological leap forward,” he sternly tells them, “be it the first telephone or carbon nanotube batteries. It seems that I must explain this technology to you, also.”

K’ler is frustrated with the distraction, but tries to get his point across, anyway. “Microchips in my head read my intentions and send them to this device by radio,” he says, picking up the disk. “It interprets my intentions as images and projects them.”

He sets the disk down and continues while the hologram follows his every move. It displays a UFO hovering over the ‘ground’ then moving up into ‘space.’ The ship turns on its side.

“As I said, the spaceship will turn on its side when it gets into space. Of course, there is no such thing as ‘on its side’ in space.”

He continues. "Each generator warps only a tiny piece of space-time, but because they can magnify each other, and because they are arranged into the shape of a satellite dish, a paraboloid, the warping is focused **through** the spaceship and to the opposite side. The right **side** of the spaceship will warp the space-time on its **left** side."

The hologram highlights the right side of the ship and shows gravity field lines, colored black, going through the ship and to the opposite side.

"Remember that the gravity generators are spread out," he tells them, "like the metal in an American wire mesh satellite dish. That type of satellite dish allows raindrops to easily pass through it. The same is true for this configuration and gravity field lines. They easily pass through it. The main purpose of this type of satellite dish is to focus radio waves to a specific point. The same is true of the right side of the spaceship. It focuses gravity lines to a specific point. That point becomes a highly **negatively** warped area of space-time, which is another way of saying that it is an artificial gravity point. The spaceship 'falls' toward it. It can never reach that point, because the point moves as the spaceship moves."

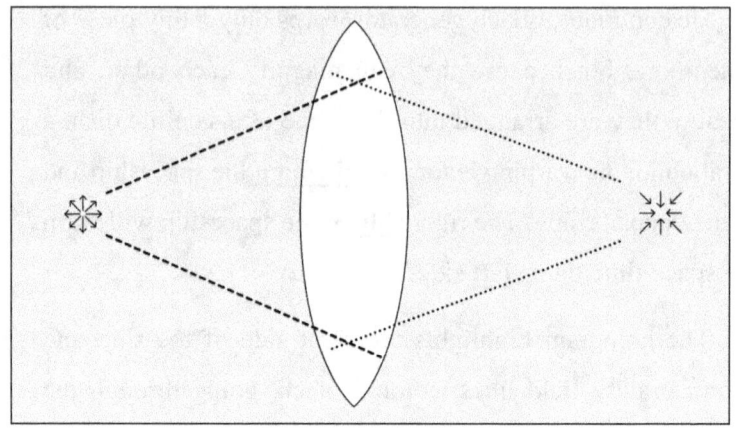

Anti-Gravity Drive

"The opposite side of the spaceship also has a satellite dish-shaped roof," he explains, "and faces the opposite direction."

The hologram highlights the **left** side of the ship this time, and shows anti-gravitational field lines on its **right** side. The white-colored field lines go through the ship and to a point on the other side.

"These generators do the opposite thing, as well, generating **anti**-gravity and an **anti**-gravitational field. Similar to the first side, **anti**-gravitational field lines are focused through the ship and to a point. It becomes a highly **positively** warped area of space-time, which is to say that it is a repulsion point."

The hologram keeps pace with his words, displaying the space-time bubble and directional arrows, each pointing the same way. "One side focuses gravity to a point," he continues, "and the other side focuses <u>anti</u>-gravity to a point. So one side pushes while the other side pulls."

"Imagine falling down a hill," he explains. "Now imagine falling down that hill while you are constantly being pushed. That is what the spaceship does."

"**None** of this is accomplished through a traditional engine. Moving parts create friction, no matter how little. Friction creates noise, no matter how little. A lack of moving parts makes the spaceship completely silent. The opposite space-time warps cancel each other out, and you ride in a bubble of un-warped space. Albert Einstein's speed limit is never broken. You can break the speed of light as many times as you like."

The pilots murmur.

Major Donnelly raises his hand again. "So is there a speed limit at all?" he asks.

"Einstein said," K'ler answers, "If you can figure out how to break this limit once, you can break it many times over. When it is done this way, there is no limit. Foreign nationals and traders commonly travel 200 times the Speed Of Light . .

. and far more quickly if it is needed."

The pilots gasp.

K'ler quietly sighs. "Getting to those speeds is not a barrier at all. The pilot simply allows room to slow down, just like an airplane lifts off, speeds up, cruises, slows down and lands."

"Like a runway?" the major ventures.

"Only aircraft with wheels use runways," K'ler replies. "Anti-gravity spaceships don't need them. They allow themselves room to slow down, much like a ship in the ocean or a train on the railroad tracks. Spaceships that travel at those speeds do not stop quickly."

Most pilots simply clap, but others are more vocal. "Let's Roll!" and "So much for Einstein!"

K'ler holds up his hands. "Let us finish the training before you start rolling!" he tells them.

The group reluctantly takes their seats, but not quietly.

After the murmuring dies down a little, he continues. "Einstein was not wrong, but we **did** find a loophole . . . and there are many loopholes. This is just one of them. This information may seem complicated at first, but it is simple once you understand how it works."

Another pilot, a short, skinny man with red hair raises his hand. "What if the spaceship has a dome on top, but is flat on the bottom?" he asks.

"Single-domed spaceships sometimes pair up," he tells the group. The hologram displays a second UFO, facing the other way. The two flat sides join together, making the two UFOs look like one UFO with a dome on both sides. "The two flat sides dock and the principle is the same as I explained before. They can now travel Faster-Than-Light."

Major Donnelly speaks up again. "If they understand this principle," he asks, "then why do it like this? I mean, why not **only** have ships with two domes?"

"Some races do this," K'ler answers. "But most spaceships land at some point. It is easier to land if your bottom is flat than if it is curved. Of course, this is not true of all spaceships. Some spaceships never intend to land, do not care about a curved bottom or prefer to function independently and without a partner. Those are usually warships, carriers, freighters or something similar."

A voice rings from the back. "Exploration ships?" he asks.

K'ler chuckles again. "I know that **your** race is new to space travel, but other races are **not**. Many alien races have been traveling in space for hundreds of millions of years.

Maps are easy to acquire."

Going back to his lecture. "Putting aside the science **fiction**," K'ler says, "some spaceships may not want to travel Faster-Than-Light. They might have a short-range mission in mind and the extra speed would not help them."

"That is the basics of Faster-Than-Light physics and anti-gravity flight in **space**," he tells them. "Spaceship travel works differently in the atmosphere, so the next part of the lecture is anti-gravity flight in a planet's atmosphere. The atmosphere of Earth weighs 14.7 pounds **per square inch**. Think about it. That means there is more than 32 million pounds of air on the roof of a small house. Flip that over and it means the atmosphere can **lift** 14.7 pounds for every square inch of an aircraft. An airfoil exploits a fraction of this potential, generating lift by creating a difference in the air pressure I mentioned. It is not as efficient as other methods. We use one of these other methods to push our spaceships sideways. Your race can use a similar technique on their highways to push their automobiles while using little or no gasoline."

Chapter 12
The Plan For Mars

Plant life evolved from single-celled organisms, just like Evolution claims, but that's not true of animal life. The Cambrian Explosion began 542 million years ago, lasted around 54 million years, and produced MAJOR animal types (Phyla). Conditions in Pre-Cambrian China were so perfect for preserving fossils that single pollen grains have been found, but no 'ancestor fossils' have ever been discovered. Mollusk, Trilobite, Pikaia, Opabinia, Thectardis, Charnia, and about 174 others seem to have appeared out of thin air. These creatures were neither simple nor microscopic. Charles Darwin knew of this, and even said his theory might be wrong because of it. Serpents don't want people to hear that part. Earth has had five Extinction Events, not one or two. More than two-thirds of those Phyla have died out, and the life seen today is based on the scant few that have survived.

Asher walks into work at the Eisenhower Building and is immediately greeted by a man in a familiar uniform. He's dressed like General P'al: black battle armor with the cape that's black on the overside and blue on the underside. He's not as tall.

The man's cape only drapes to his thighs and not the floor. *He must be in the Osirian army,* Asher thinks. He can tell by the two silver bars on his collar that this man is a captain.

Asher steps back, wondering what he did wrong, when the Osirian officer strikes his heart with his right fist, pauses for a half a second, then bows.

I guess that is an Osirian salute, he thinks.

The man stands up straight again. "I salute you in the name of the Cherubim," he says. "I am Captain T'rell. I bring an important message from L'lith."

Asher shakes the last bit of 'sleepy' out of his head. "Am I in some sort of trouble?" he asks.

The man laughs. "If you were 'in some sort of trouble,'" he says, "I'd have brought a contingent of armed soldiers."

Asher glances around to see if there are any. Seeing no one lurking in the shadows, he decides that it must be military humor.

"L'lith is impressed with you," he says. "She wants to see you."

Trying to avoid the situation, Asher points at the computer lab. "I. . . I've got to get to work," he says.

The Osirian officer doesn't skip a beat. "That's already been cleared," he replies. He steps aside and extends his hand toward the hallway. "If I may," he says, almost insistently.

He realizes that he has no choice in the matter. "Okay," Asher timidly says, and follows the captain's lead. "Thank you," he remembers to add.

Captain T'rell nods and follows him toward the hallway.

Even with the captain's word that he is not doomed, Asher

has knots in his stomach. He feels like a school-kid going to the principal's office as they walk to L'lith's newly assigned office in the West Wing of the White House.

"Mr. Asher!" L'lith exclaims as Asher and Captain T'rell enter the room. Behind her, a very large Osirian flag dominates the huge room: dolphins and humpback whales swim in a circle with a solid, light blue background. The heavy wooden desk displays marble carvings of blue whales. Its chair looks more like a throne, and a very large man stands in the back of the room . . . General P'al.

Captain T'rell salutes again. "My Queen," he says, bowing low and staying there.

"Thank you, Captain'" she tells him. "You're dismissed."

Still bowed, he backs away and leaves the room.

She walks around the desk and shakes one of Asher's hands with both of hers. "Should I call you Jonathan, Mr. Asher or just Asher?"

"It doesn't matter," he says, with her still holding his hand. "I'll answer to any of them."

Her eyes seem to demand an immediate answer.

"Asher," he offers politely.

"It's good to meet you, Asher," she says, and lets go of his hands. "I am L'lith." She motions to the corner. "This is General P'al."

Asher feels like he doesn't belong there. "Yes," he timidly answers. "I remember both of you."

"Now Asher," she begins, "You are a very valuable person to **all** of us." L'lith slowly walks to her desk as she speaks. "Your mind is as good or better than any of our best people."

Asher feels flattered.

"We want to encourage you and to cultivate those like you," she says as she sits down.

Emotion pours into him. "Ma'am," he says, "I cannot express the honor I feel right now."

L'lith holds up her hand, thinks about it and puts it down: deciding not to comment. "It gets better," she says with a grin. "As you know, we have Faster-Than-Light and gravitational technologies. I also know that you and your people have been interested in Mars for quite some time. We would like **you** to head the terraforming project on Mars."

Asher could **not** have been more excited! *An actual terraforming project,* he imagines. He had daydreamed about turning Mars into an Earth-like planet for years, but actually doing it is something else.

L'lith continues. "We will show you how to increase Mars' gravity," she tells him, "how to bring water to the planet and even how to coalesce the two small moons."

Asher looks pensive, like he has a question.

She answers him before he can ask. "Hephaes will do the physical labor," she tells him, "and no, this isn't a temporary thing. Asteroid iron is much heavier than most people realize. There is more iron in one of the larger asteroids than has been mined in all of human history. After all, the Asteroid Belt was almost an entire planet. Jupiter's gravity prevented that from happening. We'll use the asteroids, and crash hundreds of them on Mars' surface. We want to triple the planet's mass before we do anything else. Next we'll drop scores of ice asteroids, and add the nitrogen. All that weight put together will give Mars an Earth-like gravity field."

Asher seems to understand her idea. "I thought you might be talking about using those gravity generators of yours," he tells her. "Those are machines, and will require maintenance, but you're not talking about using those. You're talking about dropping heavy objects on Mars and naturally giving it more gravity. This method will last for . . . eons. The new mass of the planet will not only let humans move normally, but it'll warm the planet's atmosphere and even heat up the planet's core so it can generate a magnetic field again."

She smiles. "Precisely," L'lith concurs.

Asher speaks under his breath. "One of the many things that plants do," he says, "is turn **water** into breathable oxygen. Most people think breathable oxygen comes from carbon dioxide, but that's wrong. The ice asteroids will melt and let plants grow, the plants will make breathable oxygen and people will be able to breathe normally outside of the cavern."

L'lith stands up. "Excellent, Mr. Asher!" she says.

He gets another quizzical look on his face. "But this would take . . . well, years," he tells her.

"Yes, it will," she answers. "In the meantime we'll build a cavern out of the largest canyon on Mars."

"*Valles Marineris*?!" he excitedly asks.

She answers with a smile. "It will be like a bio-dome, but a very **large** bio-dome."

"Oh wow!" he says, trying to contain his excitement. "That thing is huge!"

"Yes," she says. "We will use our technology to make those caverns look so much like Earth that you might not want to leave, even when it's safe to go outside. Of course, you'll have smaller houses for a number of years, but . . ."

"That's to be expected," he says.

She smiles again then looks away. "In 'Stage 3,'" she says, partly to herself, "I think we will just drop those two small moons onto the surface and drag Triton over. A single, large moon will keep Mars from rolling around in its orbit. That'll turn Mars into a big gyroscope and stabilize the climate, like Earth's moon does. At the rate they're going, the two small moons of Mars can't sustain more than bacteria."

Asher breaks in. "Mars will be heavier than it was before," he says, "so your people will adjust its orbital speed. Right?"

She nods several times. "Yes," she answers. "That's easy. It will be pirouetting around the solar system in no time!"

He gasps like something hit him. "Ohh!" he groans. "I forgot about that! It'll rotate about four times more slowly. Won't it?"

She waves her hand like she's shooing away a fly. "That's easy!" she says. "We will speed it up and make it sync with Earth." She suddenly turns around to face him. "What do you think of my offer? Do you accept?"

Asher feels elation and purpose and duty and honor and half a dozen other things all at the same time. He stands at attention. "It would be my **honor** to do this for you," he says, bowing, "My Queen."

L'lith smiles. *That's better,* she thinks.

He leaves the room in complete elation. *This has been my best day EVER!* he imagines.

L'lith and General P'al are now alone.

"Was that a good idea?" he asks her with his ultra-deep voice.

She answers calmly. "Yes," she says. "This will put the non-combative humans in debt to us and keep them out of the way at the same time." She sighs. "I hate to say this, P'al, but the fate of our kind depends on their survival . . . at least some of them."

Later that day, Asher sits at a table in the same coffee house, waiting for the two girls. He fidgets in his chair, not able to hold still and looking like he's been drinking coffee all day. The other customers in the shop take notice, wondering if he is an escaped convict or a paranoid lunatic or something. The employees just ignore him.

Tex and Joanne walk into the shop a few minutes later, and he quickly stands up. "You won't believe the news, you guys!" he blurts. "Come sit! Sit!" He motions toward chairs at the table and sits down . . . partially.

The girls slowly approach the table, wary of his mood the night before, but sit down just the same.

Tex speaks first. "Last night you were crushed when you saw us," she says. "Now you're about to jump out of your skin. Have you taken something?" she whispers.

He shakes his head, laughing quietly and making a concerted effort to contain his excitement. "I've been given something," he says, "but not a drug."

The two girls look at each other, back to him and then press closer.

He chokes down another laugh. "I'll start from the beginning," he says, still fidgeting. "Last night I was crushed. I walked home in **complete** self-pity. This morning I tried to forget that you two had lied to me, but I just couldn't do it."

Joanne interrupts. "We're so sorry," she says.

"I know," he says quickly, brushing the apology aside and drawing in a deep breath. "I've decided to forgive the two of you, but things will be different for a while."

Joanne looks relieved. "We weren't sure you'd forgive us," she says. "I'm not sure **I** would have."

Tex looks at her. "Speak for yourself," she says. "I was sure. For one, he's a nice guy. For two, he's a north-easterner. They'll believe anything, true or not."

Joanne groans. "You and your 'north-easterner garbage!'" she says, turning to her. "You know you're in the middle of the northeast. Right?"

Smiling. "I know," she says. "I'm just messing with him." She sees the serious look on Asher's face and stops. "Sorry. I meant the 'nice guy part' a lot more." She takes an uncomfortable breath. "You were saying?"

He huffs. "When I went into work this morning, I was greeted by an Osirian officer."

Tex gasps. "Oh crap. That big guy?"

"Not yet," he says. "This was a 'normal-looking' guy that took me to see that big guy and L'lith herself."

The girls both gasp. "**<u>Oh crap</u>**!" they say in unison.

Joanne is clearly enthralled by his story. "What did you do?" she asks.

Asher can't help but smile. "I listened to her," he says, trying hard not to give it away.

Tex is also enthralled by the story. "What did she want?" she asks.

"She had an offer for me," he tells her.

The two girls look at each other, then back to him.

"She wants **me** to head up a project to colonize Mars and terraform it," he says, with an enormous smile.

Joanne jumps up from her seat. "**Oh my god**!" she screams.

Everyone in the coffee house immediately looks at them, but she could not care less. Amazingly, Asher is the calmest of the three now.

Joanne takes a deep breath, holds her hands to her heart and lets the breath out slowly. "You're doing it, Asher," she tells him. "You're doing it. I knew you could. I knew it!"

Still in her chair, Tex leans over to him. "Emperor Asher," she says in a low voice, "you know my real name is Erin. Right?"

He turns his head to face hers and nods.

Chapter 13
It Begins

Without uranium deposits nearby or modern nuclear testing, an ancient city in southern Pakistan shows strong physical evidence of a nuclear blast. Clay walls are vitrified, buried human remains show severe radiation sickness and the soil has abnormally high levels of radiation. Several ancient cities in India have similar characteristics. The Mahabharata, an ancient Indian epic, describes three glowing metal cities firing weapons "charged with all the power of the universe" at each other - a battle of the gods. It almost sounds like Mohendro Daro and other cities were unfortunate casualties of battles between cultures far more advanced than our own.

General P'al's silver, soda can-shaped craft streaks away from the blue-green glow of Earth and into the blackness of space. He doesn't lift a finger, but several maps and charts flash onto the viewscreen.

"About an hour," he tells them with his ultra-deep voice.

Asher looks at him. "Why so short?" he asks.

General P'al misses the point of the question. "A vimana is slow," he says without looking at him. "Their curves are not big," he says, pointing to the front and rear of the ship. "Space-time warping is small."

The flashing viewscreen stops, and he turns around.

"The course is programmed. Forty-three minutes."

The vimana orbits around Mars to its far side. A cube

hovers in space, silhouetted against the planet's brownish-red glow. Asher had not seen the cube against the blackness of space, but also notices that it isn't a true cube. Looking like a box that is over-full and about to burst, it's bowed on two opposite sides.

Asher wonders why.

As the ship grows in the viewscreen, he sees that the cube is larger than he thought . . . much, much larger. He also realizes it's not a silhouette at all. The enormous cube is midnight-black in color, looking like something out of an Arthur C. Clarke story. Amidst the excitement, Asher feels a cold chill run down his spine.

Why does this ship fill me with foreboding? he wonders.

"This is the *Ares*," he tells the threesome. "A storage vessel."

Asher, Joanne and Erin stare at the titanic vessel floating in front of them.

Erin speaks first. "I thought it would be cooler-looking," she says.

Asher feels like it's his duty to defend the vessel. "There is no air in space, so there are no aerodynamic advantages to a 'cool-looking' ship. There's certainly no extra room, either!

If you want to store something, you put it in a box. That's what they did."

"I still think it should look cooler," she almost pouts.

Asher estimates the cube as more than two **miles** in any direction. He remembers the awe and the tininess he felt as he stood underneath G'brael's giant ship. He doubts this is the only ship of this size, and now knows that G'brael's ship is fairly small, by comparison. Of course, that's like saying the Rocky Mountains are small . . . compared to the Himalaya Mountains.

General P'al is unaffected by the majestic sight in front of him, and simply pilots the silver craft between the landing bay doors at the rear corner of the massive ship.

Dim lights greet them inside the small landing bay, and the doors close securely behind them. Asher can hear air blast into the small bay. The foursome confidently step out of the vimana and into the docking bay.

Erin sniffs the air before walking to the far end of the bay. The air smells cold, stale, and metallic.

The sliding metal doors of an airlock open automatically as they approach. The foursome walk between them, and into a pitch-black room. A single, dim light comes to life directly in front of them, revealing a figure standing only a few feet away.

Joanne shrieks.

General P'al looks down at her and frowns.

"Sorry," she says. "It startled me."

Another light ignites, revealing several more figures, then another and another and another . . . The massive assembly of figures stands in formation like soldiers at attention. Their 'skin' is the color of a Caucasian man's and their hair is made of thin necklace chains, colored for effect. Their bodies are draped in brownish, chain mesh garments. Some figures even have 'beards' and different colors of 'hair.' The effect is surprisingly realistic.

General P'al takes a few steps forward then pivots to face the group. He motions toward the figures. "These are the Hephaes," he tells them. "Construction robots. They don't need air. They don't need food. They don't need water. They don't need sleep. They don't need light. They work quickly. Radiation-proof. Thirty more rooms of them."

Asher is impressed. "Even at only a dozen feet away," he tells General P'al, "I doubt I could tell the difference between this robot and a human, especially if it moves. We have mannequins that look as human as these look, but we can't make anything walk on two legs very well."

General P'al looks at him. "Two legs are not hard," he says in a guttural voice. "Humans are blueprints. Look at core muscles." He takes a noticeable breath. "Physical therapists know. Walking not a lunge. Not a controlled fall. Robot must weight-shift. Move weight to each leg. Tell your engineers."

The giant of a man then leads them to a basic elevator, taking them to one of the lower floors. "Do not move fast," he tells them. "Floor gravity plates. Floor plates are not smart. Set to minimum. They sense your presence. Increase around you. Decrease when you go. "

Both the elevator and each of the floors lack a door, allowing Asher to see a light illuminating a single Hephaes robot, marking the corner of **yet another** vast warehouse.

The single illuminated robot tells Asher that thousands upon thousands of these human-like robots silently stand next to it. *An army of master craftsmen,* he imagines.

Erin taps on General P'al's armored arm. "When can they start?" she asks.

General P'al gives her a menacing look.

She immediately backs away, puts her hands to her sides and doesn't say another word.

The group continues to steadily descend through 28 more

floors, after which they come to a very, very tall room. Asher can see the face of a giant model of a Hephaes from the elevator. As they continue to descend further, he sees the body, then finally the feet before coming to a halt at the bottom of the room.

General P'al motions to them. "Right this way," he says in his usual ultra-deep voice. Asher and the girls slowly walk off the elevator.

The girls are awe-struck. "Whoa!" Erin exclaims. "Is this a model of the others?"

Just then, another light blinks to life, revealing two more of the giant figures. Other lights blink to life, revealing even more giants.

Colossal figures surround them, each about 15 stories tall. Asher turns to General P'al. "These aren't models. Are they?" he asks, as if it was a statement.

"No," P'al replies. "These are giant Hephaes. They do heavy work. Small ones do details."

Lights continue to ignite throughout the room.

Through his White House attachments, Asher has seen big warehouses before. Each was awe-inspiring, but this warehouse is big enough to have its own weather system.

Asher looks up at a giant Hephaes, feeling minuscule next to it.

"My God," Joanne says, as if she just noticed the titanic machines.

Asher looks over at her. He'd forgotten she was there.

Smiling, she looks at him. "It's like standing next to the Statue of Liberty," she says. Looking up at the giant robot, "but this one moves. I can only imagine what it can do."

Warehouse lights continue to spring to life in the far, far distance. They can now see the vast numbers of these gigantic machines at their disposal.

General P'al turns to face Asher. "Use the Martian canyons," he says. "Get asteroid iron. Four iron layers. Put soil between layers. Squeeze until it is rock. A foot at the bottom. Build man-made caverns. Build the houses inside. Faster assembly time. Make them pretty later. Caverns protect humans. Falling asteroids. Cosmic radiation. Carbon dioxide. The cold air outside."

Erin pipes in. "How is a little cold air bad for you?" she asks. "Russians do it all the time."

Asher turns to her. "There are a couple of orders of magnitude difference," he tells her. "It's **so cold** outside that most of the air has frozen and fallen to the ground."

She realizes that she doesn't know much about this stuff. "Oh," she quietly utters, backing away.

"The surface will take time," General P'al tells her, unusually nicely. "Live underground for now. It will protect you."

Joanne also tries to flex her mental muscles. "What about domes?" she asks.

Asher thinks about it for a minute, and General P'al seems uncomfortable. "No," Asher announces. "They'll be dropping comet-sized chunks of ice all over the planet. These are **really big** pieces of ice. Even the strongest domes can't survive when something that is a hundred times the size of a mountain falls on it."

"Oh," she says, looking down. "I guess you didn't need us after all."

Asher moves to hold Joanne's hands. "Not that way," he says.

She looks up at him, and Erin quietly backs away. "Mars may be about a third the size of Earth, but it's far from small. We could build domes far away from any falling ice, but there's also the temptation to go outside, especially when the sky begins to become blue."

Joanne looks into his eyes. "You want to protect people," she says.

He looks down at her. "Yes," he says. "Otherwise we'd have to black out the domes so people couldn't see the sky, the ocean or the green plants. There wouldn't be much of a point..."

Joanne breaks away from him. "You **almost** had it," she says. "You say sweet, wonderful things . . . then you keep going . . . saying 'not so sweet' things. Ugh! You're frustrating!"

Asher just stands there, not understanding at all.

Erin steps in. "I understand her point," she tells him. "It's a **small** point, but it's a point. Think of a woman as a different species from a man . . . let's say a cat. You wouldn't lure a cat with a pizza. You might think a pizza is good, but a cat doesn't. You'd use something the **cat** thinks is good: tuna fish, a saucer of milk, catnip. The same thing is true of a woman. She likes different things that you do: nice fragrances, soft lotions, sweet words. Most of all, a woman likes to see her man being strong."

General P'al is frustrated with this nonsense. "Is plan good with you?" he suddenly asks.

Asher snaps out of his daze. "Yes," he says. "It's fine. Go ahead with it."

"Saucer of milk first?" he goads.

Asher glares at him. "No . . . thank you," he replies. "We're done here, anyway."

General P'al briskly leads them back to the elevator. They ascend in silence and continue to walk quickly back to the shuttle.

"Not good to bring females," he says.

Asher stops. "Wait," he orders. General P'al stops and turns around. "They don't deal with you at all. These are **my** advisors. They are with **me**. They are **my** responsibility, and not yours."

General P'al huffs, turns around and walks vigorously back to the shuttle.

Erin leans over to Asher's ear. "Nicely done," she whispers.

He smiles at her and the threesome dash off to catch up with General P'al.

Six Hours Later

Under a frosted white sky, two figures walk single-file, carrying a glistening column on their shoulders. Looking like beasts of burden and only covered with simple clothing, the two figures cross a barren plateau while hefting a column as thick as a man and as long as two.

The giant Hephaes robots walk toward an **immense** canyon. The canyon looks like a gaping wound in the desert, now being healed by an enormous spider web-like mesh. A second robot pair approaches the strange canyon, lugging another column. A third pair joins them, then a fourth and then a fifth.

The 150-foot-tall robots make the 15,000-ton columns look small, but the vast canyon dwarfs them both. Fallen asteroids, now called meteorites, litter the desert floor. Hundreds of robots form long lines, moving away from the massive meteorites and toward the canyon, like ants from a long forgotten sandwich.

Other robots make long 'shafts' by taking the columns, laying them sideways and welding them together with powerful lasers. They work each shaft into the spider web-like mesh, creating a tighter and tighter iron frame, like a rebar frame inside a concrete mold.

Asher sees that the columns have holes inside, making them more like pipes than columns. Anti-gravity braces prevent these enormous pipes from collapsing to the canyon floor.

The foursome watch the scene on a viewscreen from the safety of the vimana.

General P'al speaks for the first time in several hours with his usual ultra-low voice and with his strange speech pattern. "From your Asteroid Belt," he says, pointing to the enormous meteorites littering the ground. "Convenient. A blast can break orbit. Then correct its fall. Time is a factor. We used heavy freighters. These have soft-landed. These have not burned-up. These have not broken. Some canyons are big here. This is the biggest one. Brought the resources here. They have good iron. Make into iron frames. The frames are vaulted. Each frame is a layer. There are four layers. Dirt between the layers. Two hundred feet of dirt. Each layer has smaller vaults." He closes his eyes and takes another breath. "Gravity Generators. Anti-gravity Braces. Squeeze until it is rock. Build man-made caverns."

"It will be a cross between a dome and a Roman aqueduct." Asher says.

General P'al looks at him. "Domes are round," he tells

him. "This is not." He looks back at the screen.

"Then it's more like a Gothic vaulted ceiling," he offers, pushing his luck.

Erin laughs. "That's a relief!" she says. "I thought you were talking about vaults of money!"

"So did I," Joanne admits. The girls laugh. "I wondered how that was going to help us!"

General P'al menacingly glares at the two women, and they immediately stop laughing. "Yes," he answers, turning back to the screen and quietly taking a deep breath. "We will cover last frame. Two hundred feet of dirt."

Erin gasps. "Four vaults and two hundred feet each?" she asks. "That's eight hundred feet! Is there enough room?"

General P'al smiles for the first time since . . . ever. "Plenty," he tells her. "Twenty thousand feet deep."

"Oh," she sheepishly utters, and works her way behind the others.

General P'al continues. "The result is flat ground," he says. " It will look like the rest."

Asher turns to the giant man. "Why do we need that?" he asks.

"You never know," he replies. "Falling ice asteroids. Enemy ships. You never know. Hide your house well. You can do what you want."

Asher understands.

The giant man points to the columns. "Fifteen thousand tons each," General P'al says. "Six thousand tons right now. Gravity is not fixed. That is Stage Two. Twenty-five feet wide. Two fifty feet long."

Erin's eyes bulge. "That's almost as long as a football field!" she exclaims.

Asher explains. "The columns are just pieces in this spider web thing," he tells her. "The giant Hephaes make these pieces look a lot smaller than they are in reality."

General P'al doesn't care. "Yes," he growls. "The small Hephaes fix flaws. After more asteroids. We will start on Stage 2."

Erin whispers to Joanne. "Is it just me, or does this remind you of the iron bars of a prison?" she asks.

Joanne turns to her, and gives her a 'knowing' nod. "Being buried alive also comes to mind."

Both women cling to hope, but have their doubts about this project.

Chapter 14
Come To Mars!

The word 'federal' does NOT mean 'national.' The American government is just called by its original description. A federal system holds one state to laws written by the state's people. A national system holds every state to laws written by other people. The current system thinks every person is the same, which is like saying that every road is the same, so every speed limit should be the same; whether it's on a highway or right next to an elementary school.

"Christian, traveling to Mars is **easy** now," Asher tells the well-known TV host on a split-screen interview. "With Osirian spacecraft, we can get there in about an hour. With our own technology, it would take more than two years to get there! Amazing! Right?!"

The TV host simply looks at him with pity and remorse. "I hear it's a wasteland there," he says. "No air. No life. Bitterly cold. You'd better pack your Long Johns."

Asher laughs. "Colder than that," he says. "It's so cold there that the carbon dioxide atmosphere has frozen out of the air, and lays on the ground near the poles. Vapor pressure is the only reason that Mars has an atmosphere at all. The carbon dioxide atmosphere is just sublimed vapor from the dry ice, ice caps. Unbelievable cold temperatures combines with very low atmospheric pressure and the relative heaviness of carbon dioxide gas to cut gullies and erode mountains. People think that's evidence of liquid water on Mars, but that's not true. It doesn't matter, though. We'll live underground, anyway. We'll have all the water, breathable air and heat that we want."

The interviewer only understands Asher's last sentence, and humorously rolls his brown eyes. "We'll be cavemen, again!" he jests.

Asher doesn't catch the joke. "Not caves, Christian," he says. "Man-made caverns. I've seen it myself. Mars has some **really** big canyons. The biggest one is over two thousand miles long and a hundred miles wide."

Christian excitedly gasps. "**Wow**!" he exclaims. "That's pretty big!"

Asher is surprised that the graying, blond-haired interviewer has some excitement left in him . . . or is it an act? "Giovanni Schiaparelli said there were 'grooves' on Mars, but the Italian word for it is 'canali.' Add 'Americanization' to imagination and you get 'Percival Lowell seeing canals on Mars.' **Planet-wide** terraformation will take several centuries, so the Osirian construction robots are turning that enormous canyon into an enormous bio-dome. They will dig it even deeper, then put a huge roof on it. Trillions of tons of asteroid iron and soil serve as the cavern's roof and it will be filled with breathable oxygen. Afterwards, the construction robots will build human houses inside these caverns. They are extremely fast builders! In the meantime, we are protected from 'Stage 2.'"

"I'm almost afraid to ask," he says. "What's 'Stage 2'?"

"Gravity," he replies. "Gravity is the key, Christian. We're not talking about adding a few hundred tons of mass to make more gravity. That'd be miniscule. We're talking about adding 600 billion, billion tons of mass to make more gravity. With 260% more gravity, the wispy atmosphere will compact, and fall to the surface as a dense atmosphere made of the same air molecules. Mars doesn't have enough gravity to generate a magnetic field to fight the solar wind. A magnetic field deflects the electrically charged particles in the solar wind. Otherwise the solar wind will charge air molecules in the atmosphere, and then those air molecules will float off into space."

He continues. "Molecules in close contact with each other create heat," Asher tells him. "Mars' atmosphere will warm a little. The ice caps and other frozen water will melt into rivers and lakes. Some of them will evaporate, and the water molecules will join the air molecules, bumping into other atmospheric gases and warming them a little more. The

Osirians will bombard Mars with ice asteroids and nitrogen asteroids. Then they will fire enormous lasers from orbit to melt these massive glaciers of ice. Some of the melted ice will evaporate and warm the air a little more, while water vapor and carbon dioxide will give Mars a Greenhouse Effect, like it does here."

Christian looks disturbed. "Isn't that bad?" he asks.

Asher knew this question would come up. "Not at all," he answers. "Do you know which greenhouse gas is both the strongest **and** the most abundant?"

Christian gives him a quizzical look.

"Water vapor," Asher answers.

The interviewer's jaw drops. "You're kidding me!" he says. "I thought for sure it was carbon dioxide!"

"Not even close," Asher tells him. "Carbon dioxide isn't 0.3% of our atmosphere or even 0.03%. It's 0.003% of our atmosphere. Absolutely miniscule. And it's the **weakest** of the four major greenhouse gases. Earth is so far from the sun, that it can't warm our planet by itself. The Greenhouse Effect compounds the sun's heat. Earth would be a frozen **wasteland** without the Greenhouse Effect."

Christian furrows his brow, and tries to challenge Asher's

comments. "What about Venus and its run-away Greenhouse Effect?"

Asher looks at him like he's stupid. "There are at least eight orders of magnitude difference there," he counters. "Venus is much closer to the sun **and** Venus spins very, very slowly **and** Venus has 3,200 times more carbon dioxide in its atmosphere **and** Venus has 90 times the atmospheric pressure of Earth. The air pressure is so massive there that it'd crush a human to the size of a soda can in less than a second. Should I go on?"

Christian knows he's already lost the debate, but blows off the whole thing with a child-like laugh. "Well I can see that you're one of those really smart people that enjoys all that science stuff."

Asher manages a laugh. *I can't believe people trust this idiot,* he thinks. *All he has to do is look in a book, instead of believing everything he sees on TV.* Asher quietly takes a deep breath. *Calm down,* he tells himself. *Calm down. We're in two separate studio sets. At least he can't spray me with spittle.*

"It almost sounds too easy," Christian says. "Why hasn't this been suggested before?"

"There are two answers for your two questions," Asher responds. "It's easy because of Osirian technology and, yes, it has been proposed before."

"I know that the second Bush proposed it, but I don't remember anyone else saying it."

Asher knows that the TV host has selective memory, but feels more comfortable in this subject. "You're pitching to my strengths, Christian," he says. "A mission to Mars and eventual colonization of Mars has been floating around the Capitol since the Apollo missions in the 70s. NASA even wrote a proposal in 1989. Unfortunately it was a 450 billion dollar side of pork."

"Nixon?" Christian asks the question like it is a statement.

"No," Asher smiles for a moment, but becomes serious again. "In 1990, an independent engineer proposed a viable and achievable mission that would get men on Mars by 1999. It received a wonderful response then fizzled. The second Bush tried to revive it, but it wasn't handled well. The problem is that big projects take ten or more years to accomplish. Presidents come and go in that period of time, and it only takes one idiot with an expensive domestic agenda to mess it all up."

The interviewer seems to ignore Asher's words. "That sounds like Congress," he says. "But seriously, are you talking about astronauts going to Mars or a colony for real people?"

"A colony," Asher says quickly. *Idiot!* he screams in his mind. *I just told you that!* "With Osirian spacecraft and construction robots, large habitats can be constructed in a matter of weeks and ready before anyone even shows up."

Christian smirks. "Robots don't breathe oxygen. Do they?" he says, letting out another unnerving laugh. With that, Asher's segment is over, the studio's director motions for him to get off of the set and the show soon ends. After a few pleasantries Asher ducks out through the back door of the studio, happy to make an escape.

Back at His Apartment

Asher watches part of the digital broadcast of L'lith's comments on his computer. It's the part that mentions the magnetic pole shift. He does a quick 'search' on the Internet, and looks at a map of where the magnetic pole has been since about 1450.

"Records of the **magnetic** north pole have been kept longer than I realized," he says, talking to himself out loud. It helps him to think.

"It looks like the magnetic north pole has meandered around the same area for centuries. It has made a couple of U shapes, but it began to pick up speed about . . . the mid-1980s.

Since then it has been making a beeline for Earth's **rotational** North Pole."

He sits back in the computer chair, and rubs the tiny bits of stubble on his chin with his fingers. "Hmm . . . L'lith said that the pole shift will be caused by human activity, but she didn't say **which** activity. Knowing politicians, it's probably the **opposite** of what we think."

He continues to rub at the tiny bits of stubble. "I know that Earth is **not** getting warmer. It's getting cooler."

Magnetic North Pole

Thinking silently for a few minutes, he moves his hand to the side of his face, and rubs the tiny bits of stubble over there. "Humans have been using less, burning less and generally emitting less carbon dioxide, because of the 'Global Warming' craze, and it's getting cooler as a result." Asher sits up in the chair. "A cooler Earth means there is more ice and less seawater, since the ice in seawater is freshwater. Slow-freezing extracts freshwater from saltwater. Earth has wobbled for 4 ½ billion years, because there is more landmass in the northern hemisphere than in the southern hemisphere. And since ice is lighter than water, and a lot lighter than seawater, the Earth's weight will shift and the wobbling will slow down."

On a roll now, he stands up. "Yellowstone Park's supervolcanic eruption would make things a **lot** worse," he says to himself. "It took nearly a century for Earth's average temperature to warm up after Mount Tambora's supervolcanic eruption in 1815, and Yellowstone is bigger. Mount Tambora killed thousands, and crippled enormous empires when it spewed 38 cubic miles of ejecta. **That** was the biggest eruption in human history, but Yellowstone can spew **240** cubic miles!"

He looks at the map of the magnetic north pole again. "The lack of a wobble will push Earth's **magnetic** north pole into its **rotational** north pole. Earth generates a magnetic field in two ways: moving magma in its mantle and iron in its outer core. The outer core's magnetic field is the 'seed' for the mantle's magnetic field. The magnetic pole isn't physically set like its rotational pole. When it get there, it'll spin around like it's in a washing machine's spin cycle, and fling halfway down the planet!"

Asher sits down again, and continues to talk to himself. "'Water is weakly diamagnetic,'" he says, quoting L'lith, "'and will follow the magnetic field.' If the magnetic north pole is in Arizona, then the magnetic **south** pole will be . . ." He looks at a digital globe on his computer. "Sedona is 34.8° North by 111.7° West, so it'll be 34.8° South by 68.3° East . . . the southern Indian Ocean."

He looks again to check his math. "Hmm . . . Half of the seawater will move toward the new **north** pole, and half will move to the new **south** pole. Which means the Gulf of Mexico will grow . . . until it splits our country in two. The Mediterranean Sea will drain, and Japan will be completely submerged."

He stops playing with his chin stubble, and puts his hands on the chair's armrest. "Damn! She's right!"

Chapter 15
The Fleet Begins To Move

The U.S. Justice system has become so bungled that if a person kills a sitting Senator and is actually convicted, the Justice System will give him a prize. He will get to spend years in safe and clean housing without any expenses: rent, food, electricity or clothing. Even health care is free. In the odd chance that he goes to death row, it would be at least eight years before that happens, and it's closer to 15 or 20 years in northern states. An older person might even die of natural causes first. By definition, a good person obeys the rules of civilized society. A bad person doesn't obey any rules at all, so evil will always triumph over good. That is, unless the good person sees this loophole.

A heavy freighter floats in high Earth orbit, looking like a squashed, shiny metal ball. Eight attack ships are neatly tucked inside its smooth, silvery shell. The teardrop-shaped hulls of the attack ships are armed to the teeth nearly one hundred nuclear missiles. They're specifically designed launching major attacks, but can't fly into deep space on their own. That's where the freighter comes in.

Like a piece of bread from a giant toaster, each attack ship is loaded backwards, ready to spring out of its slot at a moment's notice. Twenty-seven of the heavy freighter's brethren float in orbit near the first freighter. Some of the fleet still haven't closed their accordion-like space doors, while more than **twenty thousand** nuclear missiles wait for a particular command.

"Be sure to attack their oceans, too," L'lith reminds a ship pilot. "They live on the land **and** on the ocean floor."

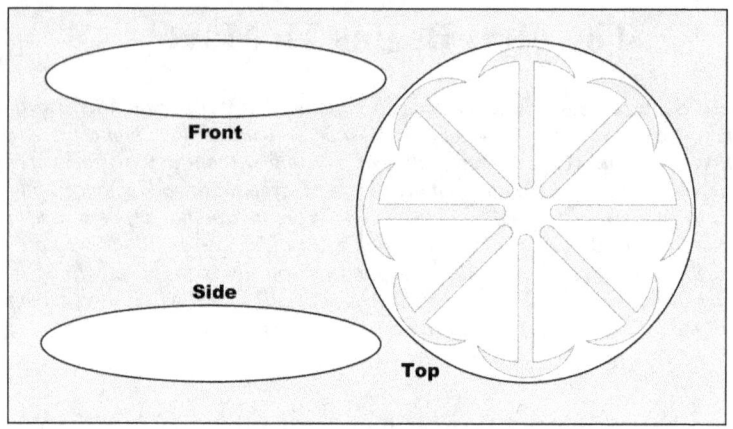

Heavy Freighter

"Yes, Ma'am," the ship's pilot replies. "I remember."

L'lith pauses for a minute, looking at the man, then turns and walks away.

The pilot waits until she is out of earshot before saying, "I may just be an Air Force pilot, but I'm smart enough to listen and follow instructions."

The co-pilot gives an absent-minded nod, then continues checking readings in the ship's cockpit.

A few minutes later, a small, silvery craft emerges from the giant freighter. Barely visible, L'lith's descent may as well have been a flea jumping off the side of a German Shepherd. The craft descends toward the Earth and disappears.

The freighter's forward viewscreen transfers to each attack ship and each pilot watches as the last of the space doors all begin to close. One by one, the enormous freighters slowly begin moving away, heading 'south' of the solar system. They seem to plod slowly at first, but within minutes they are as far away as the moon.

The Earth and its moon grow smaller and smaller until everything suddenly disappears.

"We've reached the Speed of Light," he tells the co-pilot. "Light can't catch up to us anymore. We are just passengers inside of a bullet now."

"I don't feel any different at all."

"K'ler said it'd be like this," the pilot replies.

"I know," he says. "But it's still amazing"

The heavy freighter accelerates faster and faster. The stars look like points of light quickly moving toward the ship, but as they gets closer to the stars, the points of light streak into thin lines of light, like on TV. Unlike TV, though, the streaking stars vanish as the freighter passes them. There's a reason why is called a Faster-Than-Light drive: they're driven **faster** than light can travel.

Only the navigational computer guides them now, which

reads 'Fifteen C.'

The same attack ship pilot yells with excitement. "Fifteen times the Speed of Light!" he roars. "Can you believe we're actually going that fast?!"

The co-pilot shrugs. "How do we slow down?" he asks calmly.

"The computer will switch the gravitation and repulsion fields at the midpoint and we'll decelerate the rest of the way," the pilot answers, calming down. "K'ler said this is an emergency flight, so we'll get close to a **thousand** times the Speed of Light by the time we reach the midpoint. They've made these things as easy to fly as driving a car."

"I don't remember switching gravitational fields in the owner's manual of my Pontiac," the copilot says sarcastically.

"Yeah," he slowly answers, perplexed by the co-pilots indifference. "Well . . . we accelerate until we reach the halfway point, then switch the fields and decelerate for the other half. The Osirians gave us a crash course on stellar navigation before we were allowed to fly these things."

"No pun intended. Right?" he says dryly. "A crash course?"

The pilot chuckles. "Yeah," he agrees. "The fleet

separates and comes at the planet from four directions, like the planet is a four-sided pyramid."

"You mean a 'tetrahedral attack pattern,'" the co-pilot says as he looks forward again. "That's a good plan."

The pilot is still confused by his companion's inconsistent behavior. "Yeah," he cautiously responds. He thinks for a few seconds then snaps out of it. "There are four groups: Alpha, Beta, Gamma and Delta. There are seven heavy freighters in each group. Once the group gets into position, the freighters will launch all eight of its attack ships. The attack ships launch the nukes, the aliens go 'bye-bye' and we go back home."

The pilot drops into his chair. "Simple," he adds, putting his feet up. "Just the way I like it."

"It's a long way to the Reticulan homeworld," the co-pilot says as he stands up, "and we have another fifteen hours before we get to the halfway point and switch the gravity fields. I'm going to the galley. Do you want me to get you anything?"

"I don't suppose we have any beer up here?" he asks.

The co-pilot walks down the hallway. "Not likely," he replies. "I'll need a stiff drink tonight . . . or two or three."

The pilot spins around in his chair. "I might join you. Do

you think they have any beef jerky in there?"

The City Is Almost Finished

Asher walks around one of the newly built Martian apartment complexes. They're very plain, and look like giant, gray cubes. The cavern that the Hephaes created out of Valles Marineris is larger than he thought it'd be.

Why did they make the bio-dome so large, he wonders.

They have sculpted the interior of a dome into the rock and engineered it somehow. Impressive illusions of dawn, daylight, dusk and night can appear under it.

People feel less stressed when they can see the sky, he thinks and walks into one of the apartments. *The Osirians are going to speed up Mars' day length to match it with Earth's.*

It isn't finished, but looks like the entire apartment will be about the size of one typical bedroom on Earth. Tiny.

"It'll suffice," he decides. "After all, this is the **first** off-world city." He breathes deeply a few times. "The air is good."

He jumps up a little and hits his head on the ceiling before falling back to the floor. "But the gravity still lacks a bit," he groans. "The gravity is much better than before we started, but it'll get even better when the ice asteroids get here."

A familiar voice comes from the doorway. "Is it what you hoped for?"

Asher whirls around to see G'brael standing in the open doorway. Stunned for a moment, "Yes," he says blankly. "I wasn't sure if I'd see you again."

G'brael moves into the room. "I wanted to congratulate you. Deceiving the Osirians and making them work for **you** is no small accomplishment."

Asher looks confused. "I don't understand what you mean, G'brael. We didn't deceive anyone. The Osirians are helping us to survive a disaster."

"Well," he says, "your superiors might not have told you about the deception." He looks around the room. "Small homes are fine. High populations or multicultural societies are fine. Just be sure to spread the city out, and give the people more room. Too many people living in one area damages the entire society."

"Damages?" he asks. "Are you talking about vandals?"

G'brael turns around to face him. "Oh no," he says. "Not that kind of damage. The mere **existence** of other people irritates people . . . just a little bit. Humans are more connected to each other than you realize. Similar people irritate the least, and different people irritate the most. Multicultural societies can only work on small scales. The natural Amoeba Effect would create pockets of battling factions, and that's what you **don't** want. Some things just don't scale up. Especially in close quarters, **large** multicultural societies are very irritating to each member of its population. Everyone seems to understand this, except Americans."

"Even warlords understand this," he continues. "Because there is power in numbers, large cities need to have similar people. The natural Amoeba Effect will create a unified society instead of a disconnected one. Even though there is a difference between 'race' and 'culture,' warlords prefer ethnic cleansing campaigns, which satisfies his need for a calmer society. He could do this simply by separating people, but that wouldn't satisfy his other need . . . murder. You don't want to become a warlord, so that's why I say to spread people out."

Asher nods. "That makes sense," he says as he puts his hand on a wall. "People talk about taking a vacation, and getting away from the city all the time. This city may be small right now, but it'll grow into a Utopia. No one will have to pay for anything."

G'brael shakes his head. "Other people have thought the way you are thinking right now," he says. "Socialism and communism are just survival techniques. They can only be used for a couple of decades with very small groups, or a few years with large groups. They are parasitic techniques. When allowed to last longer than that, they take over the whole country. Socialism and communism can't create much of anything on their own."

G'brael continues. "These parasitic styles of government erode the spirit of its children," he says, "very slowly. Then they erode their children's spirits . . . then theirs and then theirs. The children look the same, but that kind of erosion cannot be rekindled. I know. It's not a way of life."

He looks down. "Utopia doesn't exist," he says then looks up again. "It can't exist. It's not that we don't want it badly enough. We do, but 'Utopia' backfires **every** time, hurting the same people you're trying to help. It doesn't matter who's 'in charge,' it's Utopia itself that doesn't work. The math backs that up."

Asher smiles at him like he doesn't know what he's talking about. "We'll figure it out. Everyone here will be smart and willing to work together."

G'brael grins and lets out a small chuckle. "They say that you should do everything when you're 18 years old . . . because it's then that you know **everything**."

Asher chuckles as well and looks at the ground. His body

language says, *Guilty as charged!* but he replies, "I'm not 18, anymore."

The older man understands. "Seriously now, the first generation of you may be smart and willing to work together, but what about the next?"

"We're smart so our kids will be smart, too," Asher answers.

G'brael nods slightly. "Most maybe," he says, "but not all. There are different kinds of smart. Things like this have been tried before. What are you going to do with the ones that aren't good enough or have some sort of disability?"

Asher's smile slowly evaporates.

"Punish them?" G'brael asks. "Force them? Banish them? Kill them? All of these have been tried before. Not everyone **can** or **should** be saved, but too much enforcement and you'll box yourself into a genetic corner. Too little and you'll box yourself into another corner. People will look to you . . . personally. You'll be the Founding Father of an entire world."

Asher looks at the floor for a minute then changes the subject. "G'brael, what did you mean about deceiving the Osirians?"

Another familiar voice comes from behind him. "Yes,

G'brael," a woman's voice says. "Tell us."

The two men whirl around to see L'lith leaning on the door then walking into the room.

General P'al follows her, ducking his head as he enters the small apartment.

G'brael stands in complete silence.

"Tell us," she needles him.

No one utters a word as the Osirian pair walk into the small apartment.

G'brael turns to Asher. "My ship is in the main hangar," he says. "Could you go there and tell the helmsman that I'll be there in a little while?" He looks at L'lith. "We need to talk."

Asher feels the tension in the room. "Would you rather I just call him?" he asks timidly.

G'brael gives him a half-smile. "The cellular towers haven't been finished, yet," he says. "Have they, L'lith?"

She doesn't move a muscle. "Not yet, G'brael," she answers. "That's the thing about construction sites. Not everything's finished."

General P'al steps aside, cueing Asher to leave the room.

He reluctantly complies, and General P'al closes the door.

L'lith smiles and slowly walks around G'brael. "Check and mate," she says. "I knew you'd come. You had a chance to save yourself, but didn't take it. Why? The boy?"

G'brael stands in the same spot. "He's more of a man than you realize," he says. *And he will destroy you,* he thinks. "I've lived a long life," he says. "So have you. He deserves more than his life ending right here and now."

She laughs wickedly. "You're a sentimental old fool, G'brael," she says before turning to P'al. "Go ahead," she says.

General P'al takes a couple of steps forward and moves his hand to the mace that's dangling from his waist.

G'brael doesn't flinch at all, but takes a breath and holds it.

The giant man holds the weapon in his hand then tosses it to the ground.

G'brael is stunned and as P'al's grinning face flickers like an old television screen. It fades and the general looks headless for a moment, but G'brael notices rough, green leather where his neck had been.

His armor has changed, too. It looks more green than it

looks black. There's a sticky sound, like vinyl peeling away from vinyl, and a serpentine neck unfolds; rising from his stomach and chest. P'al's real head **emerges**, released from the force-fielded and hologrammed armor.

His horse-like head has the snout of an alligator with two short tusks emerging from the back of his mouth. There's a red crest on the back of his head.

P'al opens his eyes. He has round pupils, which are utterly black. A thin yellow ring surrounds them, and a wide red and gold-flecked iris surrounds them both. The pupils tighten and focus on G'brael.

The air in G'brael's lungs seems to disappear, and he takes a step back.

There is another sticky sound as P'al bends forward. A long, snake-like tail with a crescent-shaped tip emerges behind him. The three, clawed fingers on his hands and the three, clawed toes on his feet spread out after enduring the force-field's constant constriction. The innermost toe on each foot has an extra-long claw on it. Now free, the toe cocks up and back.

He takes a few short breaths with his natural lungs and spreads his large form – nearly twenty feet long now. He takes a deep breath and roars like **thunder**.

G'brael finds his voice at last. "A Drakyyn!" he manages to utter. "My God! I thought they didn't exist anymore!"

L'lith smiles with **great** satisfaction, "Your god, G'brael? Your god has forsaken you for more than two thousand years," she tells him. "**We** were the ones that brought the Drakyyn to Earth. **We** helped spread the Black Plague. **We** ripped apart that stupid little country that you love so much. **We** fought its creation, not the British. **We** turned federalism into nationalism, not Lincoln. Those stupid people actually believe it's the same thing. A dictionary would have helped. We even turned some of its own citizens against it. **We** are the reason they move in lock step. It's certainly not any intelligence on their part. You call them serpents, but we call them heroes. They are pawns, but those pawns captured your queen. Now the Little Ice Age can continue and become a **Massive** Ice Age. **Billions** of people will die. That stupid little country **could** have saved everyone on Earth, but now that won't happen. We ripped it **apart**."

Somehow L'lith manages to smile even bigger. "I guess 6,000 years of life doesn't teach you everything, G'brael," she tells him. "Events are already in motion. You can't stop it. You've lost."

P'al takes another step forward.

In the Hangar

"Is that all he said?" the young helmsman asks.

Asher looks frantic. "He seemed insistent that I leave," he says.

Percival is young, Scandinavian-looking and perhaps only 21 years old. He dismisses Asher's concern. "You had me worried there for a minute," says the young helmsman. "He and L'lith may not be the best of friends, but they have known each other for . . . years. I doubt anything's wrong."

Asher is still frantic. "Can the ship's sensors find people or monitor them or something?" he asks.

Percival looks puzzled by the question. "Sure," he answers. "Normally a communications officer monitors each person, except when the Council of Nine members are together. It's forbidden to monitor a Council of Nine member, but it's treason if you monitor a meeting. They take it very seriously. L'lith is the Osirian Council member and G'brael said she'd be here, so there was no need for a communications officer."

"What is this 'Council of Nine' thing?" Asher asks.

"The Council of Nine is a council of the nine leaders from each of the nine city-states," he explains. "G'brael, L'lith,

K'kul, R'ma, M'kul, A'ma and a few others are all members."

"So he knew she'd be here," Asher thinks out loud. "He knew this would happen, too."

Percival is still puzzled. "What would happen?" he asks.

Asher answers the question with another question. "Can you find G'brael and check his vitals?" he asks.

Percival takes a deep breath. "I could," he answers, "but that would be a major violation of security. A Council of Nine member has more rights than ordinary citizens."

Asher sighs. "It's that way in our country, too," he says, looking down.

After a moment or two of silence, Percival seems to change gears. "I can locate him if I think he's in danger," he announces. "Locate, but nothing more."

Asher looks up, pleasantly surprised. "Please, hurry!" he pleads. "He's in danger."

He moves toward the communications officer's corner. "Okay, now I can genuinely say that I am concerned for his safety!" Percival announces, like he's being video-recorded. He looks at the screen and wrinkles his forehead. "I don't see him immediately, but there's always some sort of interference around P'al. I'm guessing that G'brael is near him, so I'll just look for the interference."

Percival searches for a few moments. "I found it!" he announces. "If I'm right, G'brael will appear on the screen when P'al walks away."

Asher peeks at the screen, but the mysterious interference just looks like a big smudge.

"Why is there always interference around General P'al?" Asher asks.

The young helmsman never moves his eyes away from the screen. "We're not entirely sure," he answers, looking perplexed. "Which is weird in itself . . . but we think he's carrying a high-powered weapon or something."

Curious, "Could he be an android or a cyborg?" he ventures.

"Nah," Percival answers. "Those look different. I've scanned thousands of things: organic lifeforms, robots, cyborgs, spaceships, guns, lasers, computers, cell phones and on and on. Every species out there has a robot of themselves. I think it's a 'consciousness thing.' Anyway, we can detect every single one of them. They keep trying to beat our system, but it keeps beating them instead. We've never had to upgrade it. If you aim for the most fundamental things . . . they can't beat you. Always and forever."

Percival suddenly starts talking to the screen. "What are you doing?" he mutters, as if he's talking to P'al himself. "You're barely even moving."

Curious again, "What about the Grays?" Asher asks. "Have you ever scanned them?"

He keeps his eyes on the screen. "The Reticulans?" he asks. "Yeah, sure. Why?"

Asher musters up courage again. "I was told that they were all robots," he says.

Percival laughs and manages a sideways glance. "Who told you that?" he inquires.

Asher swallows. "It came from L'lith," he divulges, feeling like he's betrayed some sort of trust.

"Oh!" he says, laughs again and looks back at the screen. "That's your first problem: believing her. She's definitely a hottie but she can lie like nobody's business!" He steals another sideways glance at Asher. "That's not true," he says and looks back at the screen.

"So they're just a super-evolved race?" he asks.

Percival turns and looks intently at Asher, "They are **not** super-evolved," he says loudly, like he has just been insulted.

Asher cringes. "I'm sorry," he mumbles.

Percival breathes deeply, letting go of his anger. "No need for apologies" he says. "From a human's point of view, Reticulans are **under**-evolved. Their eyes are large because they're compound eyes. They have a heart and lungs that are combined into one organ. That's primitive and very ineffective."

He continues. "It's just like the old saying," he says, "'one bad apple spoils the whole barrel.' A single problem with the heart or the lungs, and a Reticulan is dead. When humans invented organ donation, Reticulans tried to use cattle to do the same thing for themselves. It didn't work, and they gave up. The American government has been using 'cattle mutilation' to misdirect people for years."

"A Reticulan's head only seem big because his body is so small. Their brains use 'electrical synapses.' Their brain cells don't have myelin. Myelin is like insulation is to a wire, and their electrical brain cells are like bare wires. It's a very fast kind of synapse, but it's also very spread-out, so their heads are big to compensate. Reticulans only appear super-smart when they're really just a super-old race."

Percival turns back to the screen. "Talk about a hornet's nest, though!" he says. "The Lemurians stumbled on them millions of years ago. That simple thing started a full-scale war that lasted for centuries. That's why there's uranium on the surface of Earth."

"I thought it came from meteors," Asher remarks.

Percival doesn't take his eyes off the screen. "Nah," he says. "There's only a grain of sand's worth of uranium in a meteor. Uranium is really heavy stuff. Heavier than pure gold. Any uranium that fell when Earth was still molten sank into the planet's core a long, long time ago."

Percival steals a quick sideways glance at Asher. "Mass drivers," he tells him. "Thousand-ton iron teardrop-shaped weapons covered with ceramic. They don't have warheads or anything like that. Gravity powers them. They are fired from space, and gravity drives their mass into the ground . . . hence the name. The teardrop shape lets it cut most of the air resistance, and the ceramic is a heat shield."

"Those things," he continues, "are what drove the Lemurians underwater in the first place. One or two one-thousand-ton mass drivers traveling at 50,000 miles an hour can wipe out a whole city. Hiding underwater hid them from the Reticulans, like living underground will do for you on Mars."

He continues. "Remember that humans are the smartest beings in the galaxy," he says. "Answers that seem obvious to you and me, doesn't even occur to the Reticulans. After millions and millions of years, the Reticulans **still** hold a grudge against the Lemurians . . . and they're the ones that won the war! I think they now have two full-blown homeworlds and ten colonies."

"Twelve planets?" Asher asks.

Before he can answer, Percival sees something on the screen. "It looks like I was right," he says. "P'al is leaving and G'brael's signature is emerging from the interference. G'brael is about half a mile that way." He points his finger to his right.

Asher doesn't seem happy to hear the news. "They didn't leave that room," he says. "Is G'brael alive?"

Percival doesn't budge. "I can't," he says. He steps back from the screen. "I can't push this button right here," he says, pointing his finger toward a button on it.

Asher quizzically looks at the helmsman for a moment, then walks over to the screen.

"I'm not allowed to press this button," Percival tells him, still dramatically pointing. He faces away from it and shields his eyes with his hand.

Asher looks at the screen. *English!* he thinks, and touches the button. It instantly changes, displaying G'brael's heartbeat, respiration and blood pressure.

"This doesn't look good," Asher says.

Still shielding his eyes. "Don't tell me anything about the screen," he says. "I'm still not allowed. Just tell me, 'Yes' or 'No.' Should I go to him?"

Asher nods. "Yes," he says. "I'll go with you."

Still shielding his eyes, Percival makes a quarter-turn. "No," he says quickly. "This is a construction site. It may not be dangerous to construction robots, but it's obviously dangerous to us humans. G'brael is my responsibility. You need to stay here." He walks out the door, not letting Asher argue with him.

Asher stands motionless next to the screen. As the adrenaline subsides, denial breaks down and realization has a chance to flow into him. "She planned all this," he mutters under his breath. L'lith's endgame becomes clear. "We've been set up," he realizes.

Chapter 16
The Sneak Attack

Drug cartels from Mexico regularly invade U.S. homes: Kidnapping, ransoming and even murdering residents of the U.S. Mexico is plagued with these pirates and it is not necessarily an act of war, but IT'S VERY CLOSE to one. While the U.S. government creates a true solution, preferably a diplomatic one, California, Arizona, New Mexico and Texas National Guards could put a military presence on the international border, protecting all of the contiguous American states from this brutality. The other states could help to pay for this protection. Should drug cartels or U.S. residents have sanctuary on U.S. soil?

Flying side-by-side and spread out, the enormous freighters pierce farther and farther into the inky blackness of deep space. The reality of the vast distances of space, even the distance between two neighboring stars, is so immense that a person has trouble comprehending it. Planets are mere pinpoints on a map the size of Texas, and hazards are even smaller. Navigational maps can only do so much, so a person has to fly blind.

As fast as these ships are flying, a rock the size of a man's fist can destroy an enormous spaceship. At the separation point, the four groups veer away from each other in perfect unison, like a flower opening its petals, each headed for different quadrants of the planet. Flying just beyond the speed of light allows them to outrun the Gray's sensor returns . . . in theory.

Computer control is essential. Each heavy freighter is part of one of the four groups: Alpha, Beta, Gamma, and Delta. Spreading farther apart, the freighter groups split away from each other. In the final half-second, the freighters in the group veer away from each other, and pulls hard on its 'reverse engines.' All of the freighters drop into normal space, while being evenly spread out. They're orbiting above the Reticulan's homeworld of Reticuli.

It's a peaceful, bluish-green world. While Venus is Earth's evil twin, Reticuli is Earth's true twin. If it weren't for the continents looking so different, Reticuli would be identical to Earth. The other freighters drop out of hyperspace above the planet; reflecting the sunlight, and looking like tiny flecks of silver.

The tranquility lasts only for a moment. As if the Reticulans knew about the human fleet's arrival, their starfighters unleash a fury of weapons.

The human attack ships spring out of the freighters' bellies and into a thunderstorm of enemy fire, like a mass of fireworks exploding at the same time. Freighters and attack ships alike take massive punishment.

One human ship launches many of its nuclear missiles, their white plumes streaking toward the surface. The enemy starfighters destroy many of the missiles then concentrate their fire on the unfortunate, teardrop-shaped vessel. Using a combination of energy weapons and railguns, the enemy starfighters **rip** into the attack ship, making it look like the spacecraft is made of tissue paper.

Attack Ship

Hundreds of miles from any other human ships, it launches all of its remaining nuclear warheads in all directions . . .except one. Moments later, the attack ship explodes in a bright flash of light. The blast vaporizes the attack ship in an incredible nuclear explosion. A blue-white shockwave ring moves rapidly as it expands into space. It demolishes a dozen enemy ships as it grows.

Reticulan Starfighter

At the time, it seemed foolish for the human ship to the wildly fire its missiles, but now the logic becomes clear. The planet's gravity slowly takes hold of the wildly fired missiles, becoming both their navigation systems and their thrusters.

Untouched by enemy weapons, nearly a hundred of the deadly nuclear missiles move slowly toward the planet. The planet's gravity innocently pulls them downwards, and seals its own fate.

Despite losing **many** individual ships, the overwhelming number of ships in the human attack fleet spread around the planet, like oil over water. Spinning slowly, the attack ships launch nuclear missile after nuclear missile at the planet. Seconds later, the missiles land their punch. A flash and 'smoke' follow in a beautiful, growing round pattern. Beautiful when seen from space, that is.

Other missiles reach the surface as well, and growing round patterns dot the planet's surface. The 'smoke' from the circles collide with each other and create new patterns. Are the new flashes missile explosions, lightning or the beginnings of nuclear firestorms? No longer a bluish-green and Earth-like, the planet is now charred and hellish, like a sooty version of Venus.

Some attack ships are completely free from harm, while others are not so fortunate. Without short-range weapons, the attack ships continue to suffer **ferocious** assaults even after their nuclear missiles are gone. Many captains have learned to keep one or two nuclear missiles in reserve, to try detonating them close to their own ship or to use one on themselves.

Mercifully free of the ferocious assaults, Colonel Decker

watches the battle on the first attack ship's viewscreen.

The co-pilot walks up to him. "The Beta-Four freighter didn't arrive," he announces.

Decker seems indifferent to the news. "That's why we fly side-by-side, and not single-file," he answers. "By flying side-by-side, if **one** of us crashes into something we don't **all** crash. Flying Finger-Four Formations won't help us, either. We're bending space-time back and forth, not making ripples in the air. It will mess us up. We traveled **thirty-two** light years, and there are a lot of things floating in space. Some are tiny, and some are not so tiny, but space is **so immense** that the risks are minute. Accidents **do** happen. On average, one percent of spaceships will crash into something for every 2.1 light years they travel, so we **should** have lost **four** freighters. We should take that as a sign that we're doing the right thing."

"How do we know this was the right planet?" the co-pilot asks, as if desperate for a good answer. "Or if it was even true?"

The pilot had started to turn to the viewscreen, but stops. "It's a little late to be asking **those** questions," he responds.

The co-pilot looks down. "I know," he says. "I understand that we're just following orders, and we shouldn't question our orders, but I also feel like these are questions that should be asked."

The pilot takes a deep breath. "You're not alone," he says. "I asked my C/O those same questions, and you know what he told me?"

"What?" he sheepishly asks.

Decker musters the best poker face he can manage. "He said, 'Harwell is our president, and we should never question him.'"

Amazed, Wells gasps. "Oh my God!" he bellows. "He actually **said** that? And this guy is a Commanding Officer??"

Decker had tried to keep a straight face, but bursts out laughing at this point. Something in the tactical display catches his eye, diverting his attention. Preoccupied with the enemy's movements, his smile fades. "Those guys are doing pretty dangerous maneuvers out there," he says, "and only a few are living through them."

Wells gets quiet, and walks to the screen.

"The Reticulans are not fighting for life," Decker tells him. "We've taken away any hope of **ever** landing again. They **know** they will die soon, and they don't want us to ever land again, either. There is no need for caution or restraint, since they're already dead. Why **not** fight as hard as they possibly can?"

Neither of them says a word.

Wells finally breaks the silence. "Man," he says, "Sometimes this job. . ." He shakes his head.

Decker cuts him off. "I know," he says. "I know. **<u>Usually</u>** military life is good: You train, you help other people and you get to shoot bad guys. But ethical boundaries tend to get crossed when you're the White House's bitch. We'll just follow the orders of the guy that's in the White House right now, and later we'll have a few drinks back at this pub I know. In a year's time, we'll be settled on a new planet with a few hundred acres to ourselves."

Wells looks at him. "You really think it'll be that easy?"

Decker sits back in his chair. "That's what L'lith says."

"I don't trust her," Wells tells him.

Decker scratches his chin. "I understand where you're coming from," he says. "I doubt we'll get everything we want, but I think we'll get enough out of this thing, to make it worth it. I'm sure she's not doing all this just for generosity's sake."

Wells shakes his head again. "Mentally, she can run circles around President Harwell . . ."

Decker cuts him off. "But not General Hamilton," he says,

finishing his statement. "He's a sharp cookie."

Wells nods.

Decker looks at the remains of the human fleet on the viewscreen. "We were a lot luckier than some of these poor bastards," he says. "It looks like all of our missiles have launched now. Let's head back to our freighter."

Chapter 17
The Fiery Shield

Many elected people swear an Oath of Office to protect and to defend the U.S. Constitution before taking office. Honor kept politicians honest in the past, but that's not always true for the present. Such an oath should be mortally binding in the present. Honorable actions would be protected while unconstitutional actions would, and should, be considered treason. After a trial and if convicted, the traitor's execution should take place within ONE year. Images work better than words, and that image would strongly deter any other would-be-traitors.

As G'brael's shuttle flies frantically back to Earth, a bright red star appears. Growing larger as it approaches, the ship . . . K'kul's ship, has heard their call for help.

A medical team meets them in the landing bay.

G'brael is unconscious and covered in blood.

"This happened at a construction site!" Percival tells the doctor. "He probably has internal injuries, as well!"

The staff rushes him to the ship's medical facility.

Asher and Percival can do nothing but wait. Hours seem like days.

At last, K'kul walks toward them to give them the news. "G'brael is gone," K'kul tells them.

Asher has only seen G'brael on two occasions, but feels like an old friend has died. He bows his head as his heart sinks, as though an unseen thread weighs it.

After several moments, K'kul speaks again. "G'brael spoke of seeing a Drakyyn," he says. "Do either of you know what he was talking about?"

Percival answers first. "They were before my time," he replies.

"He never mentioned anything to me."

K'kul sits on a chair across from the pair.

"It was probably an old memory," he says. "That can happen when someone is close to death."

Asher looks at the two of them. "What's a Drakyyn?" he asks.

K'kul awakens from memories of his own. "They're extinct now" he says, "but the Drakyyn were monstrous reptilian creatures. Before humans came along, reptiles were the most evolved creatures in the galaxy. G'brael called them 'the latest models until humans came along.'"

He smiles at the memory of his friend, and continues. "Pride led to jealousy," he tells them. "You see, humans replaced the Drakyyn as the most advanced creatures in the galaxy. Even though they hadn't developed space travel, the Drakyyn came to Earth from the Sirius star group in the Orion constellation. We have some ideas, but no one ever found evidence of how they got to Earth. The Drakyyn only had airplanes. They seem to have disguised themselves as human-like beings, because they told the ancient Sumerians that they created Mankind in their image."

"The Drakyyn used humans as slaves for a while but were repeatedly shamed by human mental abilities . . . and jealousy eventually led to violence. They killed many, many people . . . including loved ones."

K'kul stops for a minute, like he is reliving an event that happened a very long time ago. He takes a deep breath. "I'm sorry," he says. "I'm fine. I'm fine. A certain amount of emotion comes with the memory of the day my people died so needlessly."

Asher feels sorry for him, but he's puzzled at the same time. "I thought we were G'brael's people," he whispers to Percival.

"G'brael and K'kul are brothers," Percival whispers back.

K'kul must have heard them whispering. "Yes," he says. "I always knew I had a brother, but I didn't know his name for a long time. I was still living in Puma Punku when I first tried teaching the people living in the middle of the Americas. They were very primitive when I arrived, but they understood much of what I was teaching. They weren't as primitive when I left. They deified me anyway."

He shakes his head. "I'm not a deity or a god to be worshipped," he tells them. "That was very embarrassing. I left and took an assembly of my people to a group of North American natives. They were even more primitive. My assembly and I tried to teach them as well as we could, but they were so intent on symbols and deities . . ."

K'kul shakes his head again. "I thought a group of us would have more success than a single one, but that's wasn't the case. I gave up after that. I went back to Puma Punku to help me make sense of my failure."

"In retrospect," K'kul continues, "a single teacher had more of an effect on a group of people than a group of teachers. It takes generation after generation to slowly bring a culture up to speed. The process can't progress too quickly, or it will fail. The passage of time will do the same thing. Unfortunately, we never went back."

The wheels in Asher's brain turn. "Wait a minute," he says. "White hair, white beard, Indians don't have beards, blue eyes, white skin, deity, teacher from the sea . . . You're Kukulcan!"

K'kul sits up in his chair. "That was a long time ago," he

says in a low voice.

Asher can't sit still, so he stands. "This is so cool!" he chatters. "The girls are going to **love** this! I should have seen it sooner. I **thought** your name sounded familiar!"

Asher stops, and looks at K'kul's face. "Wait a minute," he says. "That was about a thousand years ago. How old are you? I thought you were supposed to have a big head or something."

K'kul ignores the first question and focuses on the second. "My people were wearing rings on the **outside** of our heads in those days," he says, "so I wore a hat to cover it. The Maya had never seen a hat with a 'crown' before and thought I had a big head. Primitive people don't understand what you and I take for granted. That was one of my biggest mistakes. The Spanish wore 'large-crowned' hats and even modified their Conquistador's armor to exploit my mistake. Human cleverness is a double-edged sword, and the Maya paid the price."

The wheels in Asher's brain keep turning. "One of the last things that G'brael talked about was deceiving the Osirians," he tells K'kul. "G'brael didn't get to finish. Do you know what he was talking about?"

K'kul sits back in his chair. "Yes," he says in a deep voice.

He takes a very deep breath and releases it before he begins. "L'lith is a serpent, the queen of all serpents. We thought President Harwell saw through her lies and made the Osirians work for **you**."

Asher laughs. "That's not likely."

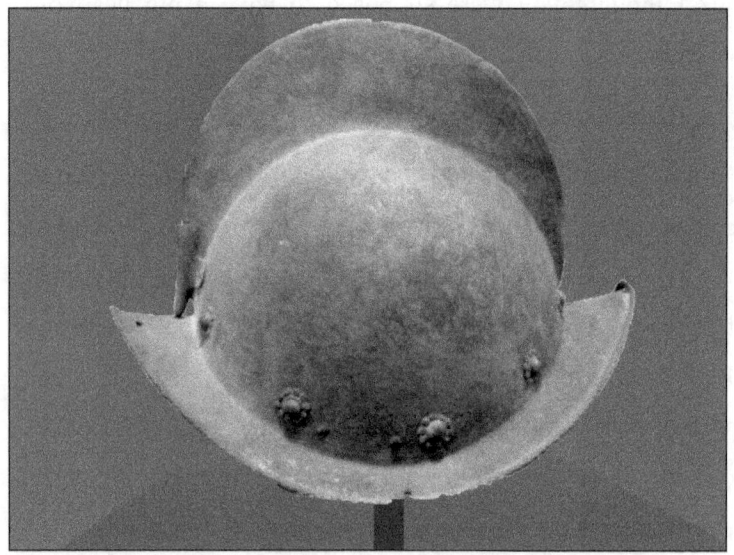

Before the Conquest of the New World Began

Percival interjects. "We know that **now**," he says. "Your country's political system, even your whole world's political systems, are heavily infested with serpents; even though your world's and your country's **people** are not. I don't see how your country has lasted as long as it has."

"Serpents lie," K'kul's deep voice resonates, picking up where Percival left off. The two other men look at him. "They lie about who and what they are. That's how they get into positions of power."

Percival looks at Asher again. "Yes," Percival says. "For the longest time we thought that you knew that the 'global warming'/'climate change' thing was a lie."

After the Conquest of the New World Began

Asher is genuinely stunned. "You mean it's not true?" he

asks.

Percival just groans.

K'kul waves the back of his hand like he's shooing a fly from his face. "Not in the least," K'kul answers. "I'd rather not tell you what I **really** think of it. We thought you had figured it out centuries ago. You closed the door on an Ice Age . . . and then this one serpent comes along!" He sighs heavily, resigning himself. "Of course, do you think a serpent will actually tell you the **truth**?!"

Asher is lost for words. "Well. . ."

K'kul cuts him off. "Sorry," he says. "Rhetorical question. Serpents lie about who they are and what they want. Oh, they speak the truth when it serves their purposes or when they're being stupid."

He leans toward Asher and pretends to whisper. "And they can definitely **be stupid**." He points to his head. "They aren't very bright to begin with. This one and others like him, convinced the world that 'the planet has a temperature' and that carbon dioxide is a pollutant."

Asher doesn't comment. He just listens.

"**In fact**," he roars, "the Little Ice Age never ended. The carbon dioxide kept the Ice Age **at bay** for 160 years! It takes more and more to keep it at bay, but once you hit a certain point. . . You were doing it."

He smiles at Asher . . . then he frowns. "Then this serpent came along. A decrease in carbon dioxide **now** means that the Little Ice Age will catch up. This was a very bad time for him to do this. That stupid serpent has doomed himself, along with everyone else."

Asher's heart skips a beat. "We can fix it," he says, almost panicked. "I can tell the President how important. . ."

K'kul cuts him off. "It's too late," he says quietly, shaking his head. "Carbon dioxide needs **time** to dissolve in the ocean. From there plankton will use it. No," he says, patting Asher's leg. "It has been **just** a deception so a few serpents can get rich. It's that simple."

He sighs again. "Throughout most of 5th Era's history," K'kul continues, "a man could get rich by hurting other men. The Golden Rule was 'He who has the gold makes the rules.' The invention of capitalism changed all that. Everyone makes money, so labor is voluntary. It wasn't that way before."

"Capitalists can lose **huge** sums of money," K'kul tells him. "Many people have gone bankrupt in the attempt, because they can gain huge sums of money if they succeed. It's a gamble. Serpents talk about the 'evils of making money' but they never mention the amount of work it takes, the lives it enriches. . ." He looks directly at Asher, "or the severity of the risks these people take."

"Serpents can't stand to see another person happy, and will stop at **nothing** to destroy another person's happiness, no matter how insignificant that happiness. It could be cheap gasoline, a cold air conditioner, the lack of malaria or even cupcakes in school." He grins at the last one.

"Serpents want to bring back the old ways," he says. "The dark ways. Serpents will help each other, if it serves their purposes or even cannibalize each other, if it serves their purposes. They have no genuine loyalty or moral compass. These people remind us of the Drakyyn, **filled** with anger, spite and venom; eager to hurt and even to kill people. That's why we call them 'serpents.'"

Asher shakes his head. "We're safe," he says. "Someone that vile and destructive would have gone to jail a long time ago."

"They hide," Percival answers.

"They're good at hiding . . . and often in plain sight," K'kul adds. "They usually take mundane jobs, but narcissism is another common trait. They might take a job in politics or higher education. You might not even realize what they're doing unless you watch them. Terrorism doesn't require bravery and they don't have any. Terrorists like them don't expose themselves to the light of truth. They hide like cockroaches. They change their names, too. They tell people friendly words while quietly subverting your society. Most people can't fathom the anger and the venom that these people feel toward Mankind, but they also can't fathom the depths of their planet's oceans or the size of their own sun or the distance to the **very next** star."

Asher changes the subject and tries to distance himself. "We ended slavery in this country over 150 years ago."

K'kul simply nods his head. "Serpents want to bring it back," he says. "A noble gesture on your part, but American slavery was the kindest in all of 5th Era's history."

Asher gawks at him. "Really?!" he asks in shock. "Are you **serious**?"

K'kul calmly turns his head. "Oh yes," he answers. "Like I said, things were different in the past, and America was one of the **last** countries to accept slavery, not the first. Men got rich from the forced labor of other men. Mining wasn't the most well-known user of slaves, but it was the most common. Mines were exceedingly dangerous at the time, and slaves were cheap. Most slaves died within two years. Not all, but most. It might be copper, lead, cinnabar or something even worse. The more difficult the mining process, the higher the price. Mining was done by hand and there was certainly nothing to keep the dust out of a slave's lungs. That's why a rich man couldn't get into Heaven. It wasn't the money. It was how he **made** the money. America changed all that. Most Americans of the past had a deep understanding of the Bible, while many Americans of the present lack that understanding. The Bible is very good at building a person's ability to empathize with other people."

Again, Asher tries to distance himself. "The American government helps its people to feel more emotion for each other."

K'kul shakes his head. "Empathy and emotion are not the same thing," he explains. "Emotion is a primitive brain function and empathy is a high brain function. You're being dumbed-down and don't even realize it. Americans of the past, more than anyone else in the 5th Era's history, saw slaves as people. Ironically, a black man started black slavery. A few slave-owners would hurt a slave, just for fun, but the vast majority of Americans would **not**. In all of 5th Era history, America had the only slave population that actually **grew**. President Lincoln didn't recognize this and tried to change things 'the wrong way.' More than 600,000 American citizens paid for his mistake."

Asher jumps to his feet. "They started it by firing on Fort Sumter!"

K'kul doesn't move. "Fort Sumter was empty," he replies.

Asher stops and stares at K'kul. "Empty?" he asks and slowly sits down again.

"Practically," he replies. "South Carolina's governor warned them that it would happen, the commanding officer of South Carolina's militia also warned them that it would happen and then South Carolina spent **two days** slow-shelling the fort. No one died, there was no blaze, the fort was completely within the borders of the state and it had no strategic value. Any other president might have called it 'vandalism,' but Lincoln called it 'war.'" He leans back in his chair, interlacing his fingers.

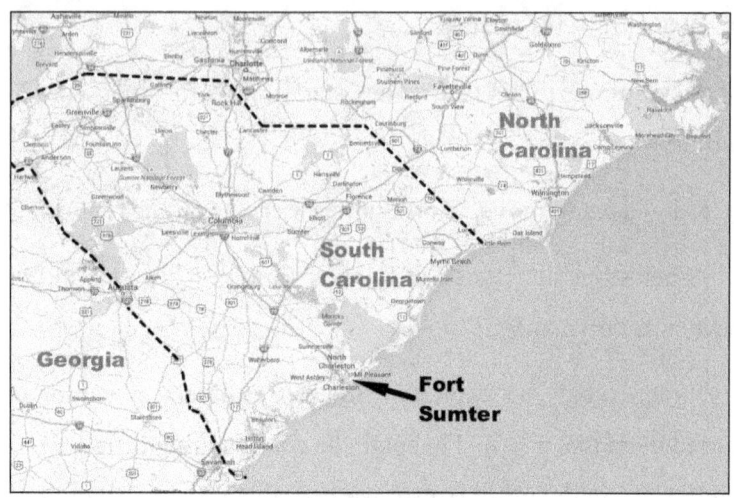

Fort Sumter

K'kul sighs heavily. "It's gone too far. Several generations later, there is still an issue between the states," he says. "Isn't there?"

His question sounds like an accusation, and Asher is lost for words again. *There IS an issue,* he realizes. His own reaction proves it, but he can't bring himself to admit it.

K'kul doesn't have that problem. "Your country needs a divorce," he says flatly. Asher is still stunned. "Bigger isn't always better," he tells him. "Split into more than two countries this time. Having two sides never works. One side always overpowers the other. I suggest splitting into large regions, let those regions become countries and let the smaller regions become states. That way you can do what you want,

260

they can do what they want and no one drags anyone down."

He sighs again and his 'calm demeanor' slips into a 'reminiscent demeanor.' "Europe was **perfectly** positioned to outperform America."

Asher jumps in. "Europeans found the 'god particle!'" he announces. "G'brael said it didn't exist."

"Of course they did," K'kul answers quickly. "These scientists have spent billions and billions of dollars on the promise of a holy grail. After decades of searching, they've found virtually nothing. At some point, they had better find something . . . true or not."

Percival answers. "Europe is infested with serpents," he says.

"Yes!" the older man concurs. "Do you really expect a serpent to tell you the truth?! It's another one of their lies! Someone who lies isn't necessarily a serpent, but **all** serpents lie. Germany introduced Europe to socialism during your Second World War and turned many Europeans into serpents. They've taken a foothold in your country as well. Leaders can speed it up or slow it down, but bureaucracies are the real danger!"

K'kul throws up his hands. "Communism will take Europe!" he says in defeat. "The French will lead all of

Europe, with the Germans kicking and screaming. Many Germans **remember** what it's like to live under a dictator's thumb. The French have not felt that helplessness in a dozen generations. They've forgotten about the starvation, the disease, the needless deaths and the conscription."

K'kul talks about it like an old memory. "The French people would say, 'It won't happen to **me**!' Then it does. Young Frenchmen," he says, "**ripped** from their families . . . only to die in pointless wars in foreign countries."

Asher finds his voice. "Napoleon?" he asks.

"Yes," he answers. "Emperors, kings and dictators; power-hungry men searching for land, power and the perfect warrior to give it to them." He leans over to him. "Your Bigfoot came from that search."

Asher laughs. "How **in the world** are those two things related?" he asks, almost daring him to answer.

"He is the perfect warrior," K'kul says flatly. "Very tall, extremely strong and extraordinarily stealthy."

Asher's smile slowly fades.

"What you call 'Bigfoot,'" K'kul continues, "was an experimental failure many, many years ago. Each Era of Mankind has had breeding programs, one city-state

competing against another. That's why versions of Bigfoot live on every continent where there are people. City-states wanted super-warriors: extremely tall and extremely strong warriors for their armies. They bred the tallest of their people and added ape DNA to get their strength. It was well structured and had very little cross breeding . . . at first. Emotion and arrogance got in the way. Once the inbreeding started. . . Well, there just weren't enough of them to maintain a 'normal' intelligence level."

He sighs. "Hairy, nine-foot tall people with the strength of an elephant and the IQ of a small child don't fit well into civilized society. They were ridiculed in the cities, so they made homes in the forests, away from other humans. Bigfoots are sentient beings but only understand the world the way a small child understands it. They are quite at home in the forests. They know it so well that finding them is like finding a Native American tracker in the forest."

K'kul shakes his head and laughs. "Good luck! You'll need technology to find them!"

Asher smiles. "I've always thought that a creature like Bigfoot was fairly likely," he says, "but as time goes on and we still haven't found any proof. I have my doubts that we'll **ever** find him."

K'kul chuckles. "And you never will," he says. "As long as you keep paying crooks to search for him, they'll keep letting you pay them. The moment they succeed is the moment 'the money train' stops. Oh, there's an honest Bigfoot tracker every now and then . . . and Bigfoot has been found many times. These honest people don't want to say that they've found him, because he is so human . . . and they know what would happen to him if they did. Just walk a tracking dog through the woods, find some footprints, have the dog sniff the footprints, then go find the Bigfoot that made the tracks."

Asher throws his hands up and cuts him off in mid-stride. "Whoa!" he barks. "How is using a dog the same thing as using technology?"

Percival answers, "'Technology' doesn't mean 'only electronics,'" he says. "It's just a fancy word for 'tools.'"

K'kul nods in agreement, and Asher grudgingly accepts the answer. "As I was saying, if you want to speed up the process; tether several balloons, each having a microphone, to a several very-far-apart trees and wait for one of his 'calls.' They make very distinct and loud calls. Triangulate it, just like a GPS, then use a tracking dog."

"But keep in mind that killing one of them is a very, **very** bad idea," K'kul warns. "Remember they were originally designed to be super-warriors. That trait hasn't disappeared. They may not be smart, but they **know** stealth. A few deer rifles are no match against wave after wave of angry and **cunning** nine-foot-tall men, each with the strength of an elephant. Bigfoots won't stop at killing assailants, either. There are a lot more of them than you suspect. They'll kill every man, woman and child in the the assailants' city. They care more about protecting their entire race than protecting their own lives. That's what's at stake. Many people have eight-foot ceilings. Bigfoots are taller than that. It's much safer to use video and infrared video. Use them at the same time."

Introspective again. "L'lith is like one those power-hungry kings," he says. "She used geological heat to power a very large weapon. It backfired and melted the polar ice caps, which were **much** larger in those days. The Earth's sea level rose and Atlantis, being an island, disappeared under a mile of water."

Asher suddenly goes white-faced and looks at K'kul. "Oh crap!" he says and jumps to his feet. "I just remembered. L'lith set us up!"

K'kul chuckles again. "Of course she did," K'kul says. "I told you she's the **queen** of serpents!"

He shakes his head. "No," Asher tells him. "It's worse than that. She tricked President Harwell into stealing the world's nuclear weapons and attacking one of the Reticulan's homeworlds."

K'kul smile instantly disappears. "Only one?" he asks.

Asher nods.

K'kul stands up, saying, "They've got eleven more. They'll counterattack and . . ." he gasps and whirls around, "and you're defenseless."

Asher nods. "I realized her plan right after G'brael got hurt," he says.

K'kul has a desperate look on his face. "This is bad," he says. "You don't mess with the Reticulans, and you certainly don't attack them! Call the White House and tell them what's going on! We need to get as many of your people off the planet as quickly as we can! The counterattack force may already be on its way!"

Chapter 18

The Counterattack

Fluoridated water does NOT help teeth. Many compounds are called 'fluoride,' because all of them contain the deadly element fluorine. Tiny amounts of poison weaken a person's will to resist, while keeping his body strong. Josef Stalin used fluoridated water in Soviet and East German concentration camps, to increase obedience to Soviet authority. In 1961, Dr. Stanley Milgram did his now-infamous research on 'Obedience to Authority.' He found that 65% of people would electrocute another person if an authority figure instructed them to do so. Fluoride's effects increase with time, and Milgram's experiments have been repeated since then. As suspected, civil obedience is much higher today.

The White House's switchboard eventually routes Asher's call to General Hamilton. "No, Mr. Asher," he says on the phone. "I cannot. President Harwell removed me from that position."

Asher tries to do it another way. "Can you tell him something, then?" he asks.

General Hamilton can give the President a message . . . probably. "I'll do what I can, Mr. Asher." he says, not bothering to write it down. "What is the message?"

Asher pauses for a second. "It was a trap, General," he tells him. "L'lith betrayed us."

General Hamilton closes his eyes, and takes a deep breath.

"General?" he asks.

The former Joint Chiefs of Staff Chairman responds after his moment of silence. "Yes, Mr. Asher," he says. "I'm here. I was afraid of something like this. What happened?"

Asher explains. "L'lith tricked President Harwell into attacking a Reticulan homeworld," he blurts. "She helped him to steal nuclear weapons from other countries, and used all of Earth's nuclear weapons against their planet."

The general is flustered. "Oh, God," he says under his breath. "Those are the Grays. Right?"

Asher nods, even though the general can't see him. "Yes," he says. "The Reticulans have **twelve** planets, General, not just one. And they are like Africanized bees, they fight and fight and fight until everyone is dead. We're defenseless now."

General Hamilton silently motions to a young soldier, who immediately brings him a notepad. "The devil is always in the details," he says, starting to write. "I didn't know those, and only knew about as much as anyone else did. They kept me out of the loop. When something seems to good to be true, it probably is. How much time do we have?"

"We don't know," Asher tells him. "Have any messages come from the fleet, yet?"

He whispers to the soldier again, who quickly goes to

another room. "Yes," the general replies, looking at his watch. "We heard from them 31 minutes ago. They took casualties, but successfully delivered their entire payload."

The soldier runs back to the general, salutes him and reports. "Sir," he frantically begins, "there's no answer from the fleet. The soldiers monitoring that 'ansible thing' that L'lith gave us, said that there was chatter every now and then, but there hasn't been anything else for the last 15 minutes. They thought it was just 'radio silence' until we tried to contact them just now. There's no answer."

"Thank you, Son," General Hamilton tells him, salutes and returns to the telephone. "Did you hear all of that, Mr. Asher?"

He lifts his head, which was resting on the control panel. "Yes," he answers. "Loud and clear, General."

The military leader is hesitant. "There's no reason to jump to conclusions," he says. "It could be a glitch on our end, or one on their end. I'm sure all those nukes going off will have some side effects."

Asher nods again. "You're right, General," he manages, through the knots in his stomach. "I'll get as much intel as I can, and contact you again in a few minutes."

K'kul walks up to Asher.

"H. . . Hold on, General," Asher says.

K'kul's body language answers the question before it's even uttered.

"**All** of them?!" Asher gasps.

"I'm sorry," K'kul tells him. "L'lith put sensors around the star system to let other races know that the attack didn't come from the Osirians. We received that information, also. Fifteen minutes ago, the sensors recorded a massive enemy fleet appeared out of hyperspace and destroyed your entire fleet in less than 30 seconds. There was no time for a distress call."

Asher's heart sinks further. "I guess that answers **that** question," he mutters.

"That enemy fleet will come to Earth next," K'kul says. "You have to get as many people off of Earth as fast as you can."

"Mars is nearly ready for people to move in," Asher tells the general. "I didn't understand why General P'al put humans underground and behind bars, but now I do. They want the few of us that survive this attack to continue to exist. I'm not sure why."

K'kul answers. "I do," he offers. "Yours is the greatest

Era of Mankind in galactic history. You are gods to the rest of the galaxy . . . even higher than L'lith herself. Your survival, even if in a cage, gives her the right to rule over the entire galaxy."

Asher stares at K'kul for a moment, amazed that humans are so important. "We. . . We'll be there in. . ."

"Ten minutes," K'kul finishes the statement.

"Gather as many people as you can, General," Asher tells him. "Mankind's survival depends on this! We'll be there in ten minutes."

The phone in General Hamilton's hand suddenly seems heavier. He hangs up the phone and sighs. "The End of the World," he says to himself then remembers the prediction of the famous scientist. "I wonder if **this** is what he meant when he made his prediction? I wonder if he'll be right."

The Saga Continues In

Book #2 - 'Stage 4'

GLOSSARY

February, 1882 - Nicola Tesla has his most brilliant moment of insight . . . alternating current.

April 14, 1912 - R.M.S. Titanic struck a large iceberg, and sank 4 hours later.

December 14, 1940 - plutonium was first created in Berkeley, California

February 25, 1942 - The Battle of Los Angeles

A.C. - 'Atlantic City'

ACU - 'Anti-airCraft Unit.' A permanent weapons emplacement used to destroy aerial targets.

Adrenal glands - Glands attached to the top of human kidneys. They not only secrete adrenaline, but they also secrete estrogen and testosterone in *both genders*. The glands are sometimes a frustration for women, because they continue to secrete hormones after menopause. A rule of thumb is that if something causes an adrenaline rush (excitement), it also causes estrogen and testosterone rushes.

Ansible – /an SIH buhl/ - 'Radio' used for interstellar communications. Instantaneous communicator.

Amoeba Effect – A common phenomenon where people in the same area, think and act alike.

Ant People – Compassionate beings depicted on Anasazi and Hopi petroglyphs (rock drawings). Hopi legends say that the Ant People rescued and protected humans while the First World was on fire. This the Lemurian rescue of humans after Santorini exploded, and Atlantis sank.

Anunnaki – /ah noo NAH kee/ - Aliens that told the ancient Sumerians that the Anunnaki created all Mankind.

Ares - /AIR eez/

1. Greek god of war (Mars in Roman mythology)

2. The name of the large Osirian transport/storage ship

Aristocles – /ah RIS toh klees/ - the given name of Plato. He wrote a few things about Atlantis, but suddenly stopped - almost in mid-sentence.

Astaxanthin – A powerful over-the-counter anti-oxidant that's taken as a dietary supplement. It works with the human immune system to prevent and even cure cancer that's already there. It doesn't work for several months after chemotherapy.

Atlantis – an ancient city that was destroyed by a flood thousands of years ago, but rebuilt underwater

Atlanteans – /at LAN tee uhz/ - Citizens of Atlantis

Aurora – /uh ROHR uh/ - the alleged name of a very fast and secret, American-made aircraft

Aurora Borealis – the Northern Lights

Battle of Los Angeles, The – Not a movie or a music album. February 25, 1942. Although it was called 'wartime jitters' by people that weren't there to see it, hundreds of people (including an admiral) said that it actually happened.

Beast of Gévaudan – The man-eating wolf-like animal that terrorized France from 1764 to 1770. This creature intensified the werewolf legend, rather than cause it. The creature turned out to be a hyena, and the pattern of killing points to a serial killer.

Beowulf – /BAY oh wulf/

1. The hero of the Beowulf heroic epic poem

2. An anonymously-written Anglo-Saxon heroic epic poem. It was written about the 8th Century A.D., set in Scandinavia.

Breaking foul – In the game of pool (billiards), a foul committed at the break (first play) in which at least three balls must bounce off a side rail. Also called a 'bad break.'

Carbon nanotube – A structure, made entirely of carbon atoms, in the shape of a hollow cylinder - a tube. The extremely thin tube can vary in widths, from a few atoms across to hundreds of atoms across. That's not much variance in human terms, but it's a lot in atomic terms. At present, these tubes are only a couple of inches in length, although scientists are trying to make them much longer.

Carbon nanotube battery – A battery under development at MIT, whose core is made of carbon nanotubes. Surface area is the most important part of electron storage – capacitance. By putting a slighter larger nanotube around of a smaller one, and then a slighter larger one around them, and then a slightly larger one around them, so on and so forth, an extraordinarily large surface area is created. It would be able to store vast amounts of electricity, for very long periods of time, charge in seconds and almost never wear out. Carbon without any particular structure is called dust, but carbon with a specific crystal structure is called a diamond.

C/O – 'Commanding Officer'

Cambrian Explosion – /KAM bree uhn/ - The extremely sudden and massively diverse appearance of animal life on Earth. It happened in both fresh and salt water, from 542 million years ago to 488 million years ago. (Some scientists say it lasted for 40 million years, while other say it was 80 million years.)

Captain T'rell – /TAH rel/ - Osirian army (Cherubim) captain that works for L'lith in the White House

Cessna - A small airplane produced by Cessna Aircraft Company. It's best-known for its single-engine airplanes.

Charnia – /char NEE uh/ - a fern frond-like animal from the Cambrian period of the Paleozoic era

Cherubim - /CHAIR oo bihm/

1. The Osirian army

2. The 2nd Order of angels; they aren't angelic

Chitin – /KI tin/ - a tough, semitransparent substance forming the principal component of arthropod exoskeletons; prior to the evolution of bone, it also formed arthropod endoskeletons

Cinnabar - /SIN uh bahr/ - Mercury ore. It is highly toxic, and often found as a red crystal and crushed into dust.

Council of Nine – a council made up of the nine leaders of the nine underwater city-states

Crown of a Hat – the portion of a hat covering the top of the head; usually somewhat rigid and gives the appearance that the wearer's head is larger than it appears

Cue ball – in the game of pool (billiards), the solid white ball that the player strikes

Cummerbund (also spelled cumberbund) – a sash worn around a man's waist. It is oten seen on a tuxedo.

Dark Energy – In astronomy, the theoretical energy that grows between the galaxies, causing them to spread apart. This is used to explain the expansion of the universe.

Dark Matter – In astronomy, an object of any size that does not emit light (e.g. asteroid, planetoid, burned-out star, black hole, etc.) The definition has come to include both matter and theoretical matter.

Devoid – Without any.

Diamagnetic – A non-magnetic substance that tends to follow a very strong or a very large magnetic field (like the Earth's field).

Drakyyn – /drah KEE ehn/ - a reptilian race from the Sirius star group. They felt jealousy and hate toward Mankind, so they killed as many humans as possible. They are thought to be extinct.

Ejecta – the magma, rock, ground and pyroclastic ash that are dislodged & ejected when a volcano erupts

Emotion – A feeling. It comes from the amygdala, in the primitive area of the brain.

Empathy – The ability to relate to another person's situation, from their point-of-view. Although it's often confused with feelings, but it comes from a higher part of the brain. This moral part of the brain is turned-off in psychopaths.

Era of Mankind – One of the five eras of humanity. This one is the fifth.

Exasperated – Tired and frustrated

Federal government – A form of government that bands sovereign states together. A federal government can form treaties and do a few other things, on the behalf of all the states, and divides power among different people. It is also called a 'federation' or a 'confederation.'

Finger-Four Formation – A flight formation, based on the V shape of a flock of birds, but adapted to fighter airplanes. It is a formation of four airplanes: 1 to the right of the lead plane, and 2 to its left. It is not to be confused with the 'Missing Man Formation,' but is named for a man's fingertips. When numerous groups of these formations are linked, it is called a 'Finger-Four Squadron.'

Fort Sumter – A fortification located in Charleston Harbor in Charleston, South Carolina. Although construction began after The War of 1812, the project was abandoned for nearly forty years, when Abraham Lincoln came into power. It is best known as the 'spark' that started the American Civil War.

FTL – Faster Than Light travel.

G'brael – /guh BREE ahl/ - Leader of Atlantis and Council of Nine member

General P'al – /PAH ahl/ - The Osirian Supreme Commander. He is very tall, speaking with strange grammar and extremely short sentences. He also has an abnormally deep voice and hides a dangerous secret.

God particle – the Higgs Boson

Grays – an alien species from the Reticuli star group

Grendel – /GREN duhl/

1. The character, the antagonist, in epic poem Beowulf

2. A modern literary work, written in conjunction to the epic poem Beowulf, but from the antagonist's point of view

Hephaes – /HI fayz/ - Both singular and plural. Osirian construction robots. There are giant and human-sized versions. Both look like very realistic mannequins, and the giant versions are 150 feet tall.

Hegelian Dialectic – In philosophy, an impassioned point-of-view (thesis) that argues with an opposing point-of-view (antithesis) and results in the actual truth (synthesis). It's usually a compromise, but it can also be a fake argument that leads to a "compromise." This happens often in politics and shouldn't be confused with debate or rhetoric.

Hephaestus – /hi FEST uhs/ - Greek god of forging and manufacturing (Vulcan in Roman mythology)

Heron (of Alexandria) – /HAIR uhn/ - a very gifted ancient Greek engineer. He is often associated with Alexandria, Egypt – the location of the Great Library. One of his many inventions was the aeolipile, a steam-powered device similar to a modern steam engine. Somehow a genius like him didn't think to use this device to start the Industrial Revolution back in the 1st century AD.

Higgs Boson – In particle physics, the theoretical sub-atomic particle that gives other sub-atomic particles their mass.

Horn of a continent – NOT a musical instrument; it is a headland; an island marking the extreme tip of a continent, extending into a large body of water (it often looks like a large, round object sticking out of the water)

Hurricane Katrina – a large hurricane that hit New Orleans, Louisiana, in 2005. The levies broke and the city flooded, killing many people.

Hy-Brasil – /HIE • BRAH zil/ - according to old Irish myth, it's an unusually round-shaped island nation that lays off west coast of Ireland. It's invisible most of the time, and only appears once every seven years. The people and their technology are remarkably similar to the stories about Atlantis.

Invisible Residents – A book written by Ivan T. Sanderson, and originally published in 1970. It is one of the first, and the most complete chronicles of USOs (Underwater Submerged Object). The 1989 movie The Abyss touched on the subject.

Jim Crow Laws – mainly in the southern United States from 1877 to the mid-1960s, laws that restricted the rights of black people and made them into second-class citizens

Johnson, Anthony – A freed black indentured servant who convinced a 17th Century Virgina court that his own indentured servant, a fellow black man, should be enslaved. This marked the beginning of American slavery.

K'kul – /kuh KOOL/ - Council of Nine member, and brother of G'brael

K'ler – /KAH ler/ - Osirian instructor, teaching anti-gravitational flight and FTL physics

Kammler, Hans – SS brigadier general, Roman Catholic and head of ALL of Nazi Germany's Black (Secret) Projects. Besides Hitler, he was the only man that knew about them all. He disappeared after the war. Although several people swear to his death, there are five versions of that death. He probably didn't die at all.

Kubla Khan – /KOO bluh • KAHN/

1. The 13th century Mongolian ruler and emperor of China

2. A poem written by Samuel Taylor Coleridge in 1797 (published in 1816), after an opium-induced vision

Kukulcan – /koo kool KAHN/ - a white-haired, white-bearded, Caucasian man ascribed by the ancient Maya as teaching them and then leaving to live in the sea

Kukulkan – /koo kool KAHN/ - The snake deity of the ancient Maya and it means "feathered serpent." Called Q'uq'umatz of the K'iche' Maya and to Quetzalcoatl to the Aztecs. It takes its name from the mythical teacher Kukulcan.

Leviathan – a very large ship

L'lith – /LAH lith/ - Leader of Osiria and Council of Nine member

Lilith – /LIL uth/ - from the Christian Bible, the Jewish Torah and the Islamic Koran. The first wife of Adam. She disobeyed God and was banned from the Garden of Eden. Enraged, she merged with a demon and became a scourge on Mankind. A succubus.

Lilith Abi – /LIL uth • UH bi/ - a Hebrew phrase meaning, "Lilith be gone," inscribed on amulets protecting a child from Lilith. She is accused of causing Sudden Infant Death Syndrome in Lilith's attempts to kill 100 children per night. Scholars believe it is the origin of the world lullaby.

Little Ice Age – period between 1300 AD and 1850 AD that was much colder than normal. Snow and ice were very common.

Lunar Month – The time between one Full Moon and the next one. (A new moon is also used.) Between the Earth and the Moon's rotation, it's seen every 27.3 Earth days.

Lunar Year – The time for the moon to revolve around the Earth once. It's equal to 27.0 Earth days. Other definitions are used, also.

M'kul – /muh KOOL/ - a Council of Nine Member

Magnetic north pole – An imaginary concept, and a convenient coincidence. Since magnets align themselves very close to Earth's rotational North Pole, so that is used for navigation.

Mahabharata – /mah hah BAR uh tuh/ - one of the two major Sanskrit epics of ancient India. It's a narrative of the Kurukshetra War, philosophical material and the story of Damayanti.

Mantle – In geology, it's a portion of the Earth between it's crust and its core.

Maya – /MIE yuh/ - Meso-american Indians inhabiting southeast Mexico, Guatemala and Belize. Their civilization lasted for 1,500 years and reached its height between 300 and 900 AD, before being destroyed by the Spanish Conquistadors in mid-16th century. The Maya are noted for their architecture, city planning, mathematic skills, calendar and their hieroglyphic writing system.

Mohendro Daro – /moh HEN droh • DAR oh/ - a city in ancient Pakistan that shows evidence of intense heat and radiation, as if it had been the site of a nuclear explosion thousands of years ago

Molluska – freshwater and marine animals from the Cambrian period of the Paleozoic era. They are still alive today in the form of clams and oysters.

Mount Tambora – A supervolcano in Indonesia. It erupted in early April of 1815, causing the infamous 'Year Without A Summer.'

Naga – /nah GAH/ - According to the Mahabharata of ancient India, they were people with both human and serpent traits. They were the deserving victims of Garuda, the bird-like creature flown by Vishnu.

National government – A single, sovereign government that governs a single nation. This is the typical form. The larger it gets (population), the more likely corruption flourishes.

Neural Omission – a method to remove a thought from a person's mind

Neutrino – /noo TREE noh/ - In particle physics, a theoretical sub-atomic particle that is electrically neutral and super-light (undetectable)

Olophagus – /oh loh FAY gus/ - Greek word meaning, "swallows whole." A dragon that terrorized medieval Poland.

Opabinia – /oh puh BIN ee uh/ - a marine animal with five eyes, a V-shaped tail and a trunk-like/mantis-like stalk, from the Cambrian period of the Paleozoic era

Order of Magnitude – Ten times whatever you're talking about. If something is twice as big, it's not even one order of magnitude, but if something is 1,000 times as big then it's three orders of magnitude.

Osiria – /oh SEER ee uh/ - home of the enemy of ancient Atlantis. It was destroyed in ancient times, but rebuilt underwater. The Ancient Egyptians called it 'Osiris,' and thought of it as a single person and worshipped it as a god. He is a green-skinned and bearded god of the underword. (Under the world)

Overton Window – In politics, the range of ideas that the public will accept – the public's 'window.' This range is manipulated by religion, community values, national pride, public policy, etc.

PC – 'Politically Correct'

Papal bull – /pay PUL • BUHL/ - a formal, written proclamation from the Pope (sealed with a leaden bulla)

Panspermia – A theory that tries to explain the Cambrian Explosion (of animal life). It says that the 'ancestors' of animal life originated in outer space, and populated the early Earth when conditions were favorable. It doesn't explain why it stopped - why did it only happen at that point in time? Also, why does no evidence exist? These simple questions and other make the theory fall apart.

Pauldron - /PAHL drahn/

1. When used with a cape, it's a decorative guard that covers both shoulders and holds the cape. This type is usually ceremonial.

2. When used on plate armor, it's a steel guard that covers one of the shoulders. This type is for defense against right-handed or left-handed attacks from a specific type of weapon, so the pauldrons on each shoulder are rarely symmetrical.

3. Sometimes both plate armor and a cape are used together.

Percival – A young, Scandinavian-looking Atlantean helmsman. He primarily works for K'kul, but occasionally for G'brael.

Permian Mass Extinction – A mass extinction that occurred 252.2 million years ago. (Caused by the Lemurian-Reticulan war.) It was the greatest mass extinction event in Earth's history. Also called the Permian-Triassic Extinction Event, and The Great Dying.

Phyla – /FI luh/ - Plural of the word 'phylum.' The 2nd level (of 7 levels) of biological classification: Kingdom, Phylum, Class, Order, Family, Genus and Species.

Pidima – /PID ee muh/ - Greek word meaning, "to bounce." Evasive maneuver that dodges incoming projectiles.

Pikaia – /pih KI uh/ - a marine animal from the Cambrian period of the Paleozoic era. Although it didn't have a well-defined head, it looked like a cross between a leech and a fish. It was one of the first animals to have a backbone.

Puma Punku – /POO muh • POON koo/ - A remarkably advanced archaeological site in Bolivia (central South America). The stones are extremely hard, while having deep and incredibly symmetric details. The stones also use a very sophisticated interlocking system. It was used for a long time, then destroyed by its own builders. The date of Puma Punku's construction is still hotly debated.

Quadrant – one-fourth of something

R'ma – /ruh MAH/ - a Council of Nine Member

Railgun – an electrically powered artillery gun that accelerates a conductive projectile along electromagnetic rails. It only uses electrical energy to propel the projectile, which travels much faster than firearm technology allows.

Rails – in the game of pool (billiards), the side wall of the tabletop

Reticulan – /re TIK yu Luhn/ - An extraterrestrial alien. A Gray.

Reticuli – /re TIK yu lie/ - the Grays' homeworld

Revolution – In physics, when something (a planet, for example) goes around something else (the sun, for example). It's also called an orbit.

Ring of Solomon – King Solomon was given a 'ring' to give him access to wisdom and knowledge, and he wore the ring on his head. That's where a crown comes from. In ancient times, people referred to an angel's halo as a 'Ring of Solomon.' In modern times, that device is implanted inside a person's head.

RIO – /REE oh/ - Radio Intercept Officer. The navigator in a two-man military jet.

Rotation – In physics, when something spins in a circle (a planet, for example), like a top spins

Rotational North Pole – the extreme top of 'the invisible stick' upon which any planet rotates (not revolves)

S'lon – /suh LAHN/ - a human android of Atlantean design

SAM – /SAM/ - Surface-to-Air-Missile.

Schliemann, Heinrich – German amateur archaeologist who used Homer's epic, Iliad, to uncover the ancient city of Troy in 1868

Sentient – /sen TEE ent/ - consciousness or self-awareness

Seraphim - /SAR uh fim/

1. The "Atlantean" army.

2. The 1st Order of angels. (They are classic angels.)

Serpent – A human of either gender, bent on harming other humans (plural). A human traitor to Mankind. They are reminiscent of the Drakyyn in the hatred they feel toward humans.

Shoot (a cue ball) – in the game of pool (billiards), striking the cue ball with a poolstick

Solar Year – time period equal to 365.25 Earth days

Sophist – /SOH fist/ - a "wise man" in ancient Greece. He is usually a teacher and/or an author.

Sporadically – occasionally

Stannum – /STAN num/ - a silvery alloy that is used both to significantly repel seawater from spaceships and to make anti-gravity generators

Stella Kowalski – one of the three main characters in Tennessee Williams' screenplay "A Streetcar Named Desire". In the 1951 movie, Kim Hunter played her, alongside Marlon Brando and Vivien Leigh.

Sublime – In chemistry, a somewhat strange melting process where a solid state of matter melts directly into its gaseous state. This is because the air pressure is too low to allow its liquid state. This is most often seen when dry ice sublimes into carbon dioxide gas.

Supervolcano – Any volcano capable of erupting more than 1015 kilograms of ejecta. (1,000,000,000,000,000 kilograms of earth and rock is approximately equal to 2 miles of earth and rock.) There are only a handful of these in the world.

Tesla Coil – A mostly-spherical, resonant transformer circuit (lightning generator) invented by Nicola Tesla around 1891

Thectardis – /thek TAR dis/ - a marine animal from the Cambrian period of the Paleozoic era and looked like an inverted cone. It did not seem to attach to anything or dig, apparently preferring to 'move around' on the tip of its body and opposite of a snail.

Theropod – A three-toed, carnivorous dinosaur. There are the ancestors of modern birds.

Trilobite – /TRI loh bit/ - a marine animal, resembling a cross between a roly-poly bug and a horseshoe crab, from the Cambrian period of the Paleozoic era.

Troy – the ancient city that was made famous by Homer's epic, Iliad, the Trojan War and the Trojan Horse

T. Rex (*Tyrannosaurus rex*) – a carnivorous, Theropod dinosaur that lived between 67 million years ago and 65.5 million years ago, during the late Cretaceous Period

Umbra – The darkest part of a shadow. The penumbra and the antumbra being the other two parts.

Valles Marineris – An enormous valley on Mars, 2,500 miles long, 120 miles at it widest and 20,000 feet at its deepest, near the equator.

Vapor pressure – In chemistry, a thermodynamic equilibrium with a compound's condensed phase. (For example, liquid water has a certain vapor pressure with evaporated water, at a given temperature.)

Vimina – /vee MAH nuh/

1. In ancient times, a wingless aerial craft made famous by the Indian epic, Mahabharata. The modern craft bears the same name.

2. In modern times, a small aerial craft without wings, soda-can-shaped and silver

Vishnu – /VISH noo/ - is the supreme God in the Vaishnavite tradition of Hinduism

Vitrification – /vih trih fih KAY shun/ - Conversion of rocky or clay substances into a glazed, glass-like material. It's usually done with extreme heat and somewhat resembles the effects of a kiln on ceramics, but to a much greater extent.

Whiteman Air Force Base – an Air Force base in Kansas City, Missouri, where most of the B-2 Stealth Bombers are based

Wow! Signal – in August of 1977, within 4 years of using the Big Ear radio telescope, scientists searching for an alien signal, detected a very intense interstellar radio signal that lasted for a full 72 seconds. Its origin (a small area in the Sagittarius Constellation) has been scanned many times, but the radio signal has vanished.

Year Without A Summer – The summer (actually the whole year) of 1816. During the Little Ice Age, the supervolcano, Mount Tambora in Indonesia, erupted in April of 1815. The global effect wasn't felt until 1816. Amidst crop failures, starvation and snow for an entire year; Mary Shelley wrote the book <u>Frankenstein</u>, rich with themes of ice and snow.

Yellowstone Caldera – A caldera (depression of a volcano's mouth) located in Yellowstone National Park. It is 34 miles by 45 miles.

Zeta-2 Reticuli – A white, main sequence star in the Reticulum constellation ("The Net"), and the companion star (a binary solar system) of Zeta-1 Reticuli. The star is remarkably similar to the Sun and has been suspected of having planets in 'The Habitable Zone.'

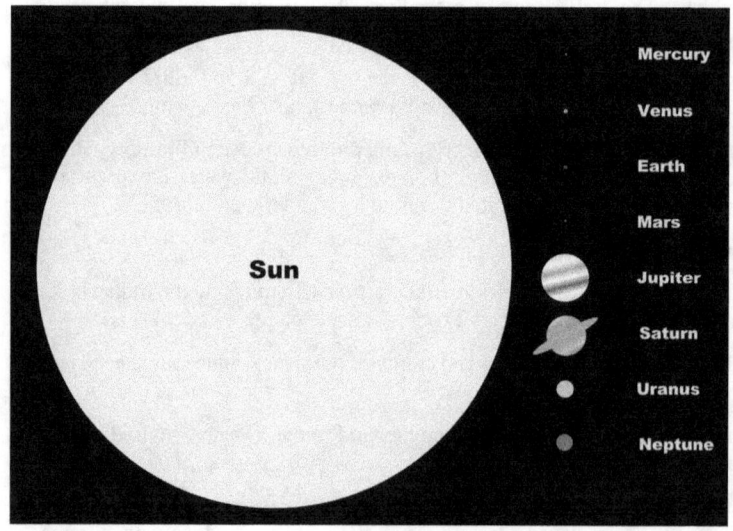

(To Scale)

"By the skillful and <u>sustained</u> use of propaganda, one can make a people see even heaven as hell, or an extremely wretched life as paradise."

- Adolf Hitler

"If you like your health insurance, you can keep it."
"If you like your health insurance, you can keep it."
"If you like your health insurance, you can keep it."
"If you like your health insurance, you can keep it."

- Barack Obama

"What good fortune for governments that the people do not think."

- Adolf Hitler

"We have to pass the bill [Obamacare] so that you can find out what is in it."

- Nancy Pelosi

OTHER BOOKS BY THIS AUTHOR

- The Republic of Mars: Stage 4 (Book 2)
Novel - English

- The Oyster Coast
Short Story - English

- Die Auster Küst von Texas
Short Story - German

- How NOT To Find Bigfoot
Short Story - English

- Wie NICHT zu Big Foot finden
Short Story - German

- How To Spot A Bigfoot Hoax
Short Story – English

ABOUT THE AUTHOR

Matthew B. Thompson is a native Texan and an avid fan of science, science-fiction and history. He has a background in physics and biology with a very good understanding of engineering and evolutionary genetics. He earned the rank of Eagle Scout at a young age, but was stricken with a very serious tumor shortly after earning a Bachelor of Science degree.

He beat the odds, even though he had less than a 1% chance of survival. To shock his doctors even further ... he started walking again. To EVERYONE'S amazement ... he got married. He is now the stay-at-home father for their small child.

Follow Him On Facebook!